"Why'd you disappea...

Frank stared off toward the window for a moment and then looked back at April. "Why'd you cheat?"

The words hit her like sharp, jagged rocks being thrown. He thought she'd cheated?

How could he possibly think that? What had she ever done that would have led him to believe something so false?

Hope rushed out of her, like air from a rapidly deflating balloon. "How could you say that?"

He opened his mouth like he was going to speak, then closed it again and looked away.

Dozer came over and stood beside Frank, whining a little.

She was supposed to be strong and independent. She ought to stand up and walk away.

But her legs felt too weak, her heart too empty. That brief moment of having him again, thinking it could possibly work between them, had made his harsh words all the more bruising.

Her phone buzzed, distracting her from the pain. Reflexively, she apologized. "I'm sorry, I have to get that. It might be about the twins."

The twins who are your kids.

Lee Tobin McClain is the *New York Times* bestselling author of emotional small-town romances featuring flawed characters who find healing through friendship, faith and family. Lee grew up in Ohio and now lives in Western Pennsylvania, where she enjoys hiking with her goofy goldendoodle, visiting writer friends and admiring her daughter's mastery of the latest TikTok dances. Learn more about her books at www.leetobinmcclain.com.

Books by Lee Tobin McClain

Love Inspired

K-9 Companions

Her Easter Prayer
The Veteran's Holiday Home
A Friend to Trust
A Companion for Christmas
A Companion for His Son
His Christmas Salvation
The Veteran's Valentine Helper

Rescue Haven

The Secret Christmas Child
Child on His Doorstep
Finding a Christmas Home

Redemption Ranch

The Soldier's Redemption
The Twins' Family Christmas
The Nanny's Secret Baby

Visit the Author Profile page
at LoveInspired.com for more titles.

THE VETERAN'S VALENTINE HELPER

LEE TOBIN McCLAIN

Love Inspired
INSPIRATIONAL ROMANCE

LOVE INSPIRED®
INSPIRATIONAL ROMANCE

Recycling programs
for this product may
not exist in your area.

ISBN-13: 978-1-335-90473-7

The Veteran's Valentine Helper

Love Inspired
22 Adelaide St. West, 41st Floor
Toronto, Ontario M5H 4E3, Canada
www.LoveInspired.com

Printed in U.S.A.

And ye shall know the truth,
and the truth shall make you free.
—*John* 8:32

To imperfect moms of imperfect kids everywhere.

Chapter One

April Collins parked in front of her new temporary home, yawned and stretched tired muscles. Driving all night had been best for her six-year-old twins, but she was exhausted.

She looked up at the blue sky and thanked God for a sunny day and a truck that had made it from Chicago to Western Pennsylvania.

A fresh start for the new year. She'd grown up here in Holiday Point, rebelled and gotten her heart broken here, and had escaped the town eagerly. Now she hoped it would be a refuge.

The carriage house in front of her was made of old white brick with blue trim. Foot-long icicles hung from the gutters, and just past the tree-lined backyard, she caught a glimpse of the sparkling river. Way more charming than the run-down apartment they'd left behind.

Attached to one end of their new home was the main house, where her employer would be living. Scarily enough, they'd be sharing a kitchen, dining room and living room. She hoped he liked kids.

"We get to live *here*?" Evelyn asked from the back seat. For once, she sounded the way a six-year-old should: happy and filled with wonder.

"Where?" Eli, Evelyn's twin, let out an audible yawn. When April looked back, Evelyn had already unfastened her seat belt and climbed out of her booster seat. She assisted her brother with the same task.

"We're in Holiday Point, where I grew up, and we do get to live here for a little while. Come on, let's look inside before we start unloading boxes." April climbed out and helped the twins down from the high seat, then made sure they were stable on the icy, rocky twin path of a driveway.

The three of them hurried to the house, their breath making clouds in the cold morning air. April punched in the code she'd been given, opened the oak-plank front door and made the twins wipe their feet. Then she let them run inside.

As they pushed through the door that led to the private part of the carriage house and raced upstairs to see the bedrooms, April walked around the partially furnished main floor, assessing how well the shared space would fit their needs. If she could move the table into the kitchen, she and her employer could use the dining room for an office.

She moved to the window and looked out at the river, racing its sun-spangled way down to the point for which Holiday Point was named.

"Mom! We picked our room!" Footsteps thundered down the stairs, and then each twin grabbed her by a hand and tugged at her.

She let them lead her upstairs, smiling at their enthusiasm.

April had been uneasy about their city neighborhood for the past six months, had scanned job listings elsewhere, especially looking in the general vicinity of Holiday Point, where she still had a few relatives. But it was a rural area, and she'd found no jobs that fit.

And then one day she'd gotten stuck in city traffic and been a minute late to pick up the twins from the kindergarten bus. When she'd reached the bus stop, the twins had been chatting with a scary-looking man in a suit, who'd disappeared immediately when April rushed up.

She'd panicked.

Of course, she'd chided the twins for ignoring her lessons about stranger danger, and they'd promised to do better. But they were little, and she couldn't trust them to remember about safety.

That night, she'd stayed up searching job postings and rentals, praying for a pathway to a safer life for her children. In the morning, a new position had appeared on her job feed: *Freelance writer to help veteran with true-crime story.*

God had been looking out for her, preparing her, when He'd prompted her to turn her interest in writing into a side hustle, creating content for parenting and child care blogs. She'd even written a couple of articles about parenting for military and law-enforcement websites, and that was what had convinced the hiring agency to offer her this new job.

"We want *this* room," Eli said, gesturing toward the room on the right.

She followed the twins into the room and her heart swelled with happiness. It was adorable, with a twin bed on each side and a big window facing out onto the street. Slanted ceilings came to a peak at the center. The walls were a cheerful blue with white trim.

"Our dresser can go here," Evelyn said, indicating a spot by the door. "And there's a closet to hang things up. We'll keep it clean if we can stay." She turned anxious eyes up to her mother.

April's heart nearly broke at this further evidence that the twins hadn't been happy in their former neighborhood. "Of course you will. You're both good helpers. And this looks like the perfect room for you."

The twins hugged each other. "We gotta get our boxes and unpack," Evelyn told Eli, taking the motherly tone she'd been using lately. "We have to find our good clothes to wear tomorrow."

"Tomorrow's just the tour of the school," April reassured her. "But it's a great idea to get our boxes and unpack. We'll make the beds and you can choose what to wear, tomorrow and then the next day, when you'll start school."

Evelyn looked rapturous. Eli's forehead

wrinkled and the corners of his mouth turned down. School was hard for him.

She knelt down and hugged both of them. "I've heard your new teacher is very nice."

The town of Holiday Point was visible from the window, and looking over her children's shoulders, April was flooded with memories. Playing on the sidewalks, walking to the shops with friends, strolling to the park hand in hand with—

"Come see *your* room," Evelyn urged.

Thankful for the distraction, April followed her. She was game to sleep anywhere, as long as her kids were happy and safe. But the little bedroom in the back of the house was really pretty. The same slanted ceilings, but this room was painted dove gray, with a view of icy tree branches framing the river, and featured a double bed, closet, dresser and bookshelf.

April let out a breath she felt like she'd been holding since she'd left Holiday Point seven years ago. It was surprisingly good to come home.

They made short work of bringing in the boxes labeled *bedroom*, and April supervised the kids in unpacking a box each. Even though her six-year-olds' unpacking and organizing skills were minimal, April was committed to teaching them to work and help at home.

When Eli tugged at her, though, and Evelyn asked if they could go outside, she agreed. "Just in the yard," she said, "and put on your boots first."

She watched through the window as they ran outside, her heart constricting with love. What a blessing they were. What a blessing this opportunity was. She would make the most of it.

Which meant she'd better set up the office first. Her initial meetup with her co-writer was to begin soon, even though it was New Year's Day. The agent had warned her that this was a rush job, with work to do every day except Sundays for the entire six weeks.

It was going to be a challenge with the

twins. But she was determined to figure it out. She'd get them settled in school, and then follow up with a couple of her cousins about Saturday activities for kids.

This incredible gig in her hometown would allow her to get settled and find more work, see if she could make a viable business of freelancing. There was even another writer in town, a blogger named Jodi, whose work April had been following. She hoped the woman would be as friendly in person as she'd been online.

She set up her desk and computer, keeping an eye on the twins as they rushed around the yard, exploring and shouting. Being kids. Free to play. Not worrying about dangerous strangers.

After checking the time, she walked outside and sat on the sunny porch steps, bundled in her down jacket, listening to the twins describe all they'd found.

A car pulled into the driveway of the big house, and hope warred with nerves inside her. Time to meet the man with whom she'd be working closely for the next six weeks. This could be great, or...not.

"Run along now," she said to the twins. "Stay where you can see me."

They lingered, clinging.

"Is that a blue jay I see?" she asked, pointing.

Evelyn rushed off to explore, with Eli following.

April turned toward the car and gave a friendly wave. And then her hand slowed and dropped to her side. She squinted. Was that...? No. Trick of the light.

The car parked and the driver got out, then ran his hand over the top of his head in a characteristic move that April had never forgotten. She sucked in a breath and put a hand to her racing heart, nearly bowled over by discordant, clanging emotions from the past.

Walking toward her, leaning a little on a large, harnessed dog, was Frank Wilkins. The man who'd ghosted her before she'd even known ghosting was a thing.

She tried to slam a mental door against remembered teenage, pregnancy-hormone-induced feelings. Panic. Hurt. Insecurity.

She sucked in a breath and looked over at her twins, now building a six-year-old's version of a snow fort. They were her reasons for keeping it together. The reason she'd handle this unexpected and awful development, just like she handled everything. A single mom didn't have a choice.

She squared her shoulders and watched him approach, this man who was even better looking than he'd been seven years ago.

You can do this. You have to do this.

What had happened to Frank, the biggest linebacker in the history of the Holiday Point schools, the kid who'd notoriously turned down a couple of Division I football scholarships in order to go to war? Why was he leaning on a dog in a service vest?

All of those swirling thoughts about her first love, now her employer, settled as the biggest truth about Frank took center stage in her mind.

It wasn't the fact that he'd abandoned her and explicitly told his family not to give her any contact information. It was that, unbeknownst to them, and maybe to him, he was the father of her twins.

Frank Wilkins walked toward the carriage house on the property his agent had rented for him. He looked at the woman standing in front of it.

Blinked. Looked away. Looked again.

April Collins. The long-legged, long-haired waif who'd stolen his heart when he was twenty-five and she was barely eighteen.

Blood pounded in his ears, the same steady drumbeat of hurt and rage he'd felt when he'd learned what she'd done seven years ago. His face hot, his muscles tight, he walked slowly closer.

He should thank her for teaching him not to give his heart to anyone. The lesson had come too late to halt his feelings for her, but he'd followed it carefully ever since.

Now he could see that she'd gone white. Her eyes looked huge in that makeup-free face. She twisted one sneaker-clad foot behind the other.

She didn't look a day over eighteen, though she had to be, what, twenty-five? Just the age he'd been when...

Why on earth hadn't he vetted the co-writer beforehand?

He stumbled a little and leaned heavily on Dozer. The rottweiler didn't flinch, just plodded on more slowly like the construction vehicle he'd been named for.

Frank's disability was why he had left everything in his pushy agent's hands. He'd been in Mexico City for a promising vestibular treatment that ultimately hadn't worked.

He stopped six feet in front of her. "Didn't you get my name?"

"No," she said, and he could tell with just that one syllable that her voice was still the same husky, smoky tone that had once driven him wild. "Your agent only gave me your pseudonym. She seemed worried about security."

Frank rolled his eyes and was rewarded with a dizzy sensation. He gripped Dozer's harness tighter. "It's because of the subject matter, which I'm sure LaWanda told you about." He studied her. "Aside from obvious personal issues, are you up to working on this kind of project? The content can get pretty rough."

Her eyebrow lifted, just a fraction, and he read her unspoken message. She was tiny and looked fragile, but she was tough. Had been even back in her teens, thanks to her police chief father. "I'm fine with it," she said.

But Frank wasn't fine with all of this, and he'd better let her know that immediately, before she settled into the role. "I'm sorry, April, I'm sure you're as good as LaWanda says you are, writing-wise, but I just don't think I can work with you." There. He'd been civil enough.

She looked down, and then glanced

toward the river, and then met his eyes. "At least let me tell you about my qualifications," she said. "I've done a lot of freelance writing in the past four years, including some work for a police department. I've also collaborated on a book, so I'm familiar with longer—"

"Why would you even want to work with me?" he interrupted her, hearing the roughness in his own voice.

She didn't pretend not to understand. "I know it's awkward—"

"Awkward?" he burst out. "Is that what you call it?"

"Frank," she said, and the sound of his name in that smoky voice silenced him. She propped a hand on a slender hip. "That's the second time you've interrupted me. If we're to work together, you'll need to stop doing that."

"With all your *talents*," he said, leaning sarcastically on the last word, "I'm sure you have your choice of jobs." *Just like you had your choice of men.* Was she still with the guy she'd left him for?

"Actually, no," she said. "We've started moving in, and the kids are all set up to enroll in school tomorrow. So it won't be easy to pivot."

"You did all that before even meeting with me once? Why would you do that?"

"Um… I was desperate?" She said the words with a humorless smile.

Only then did he really register the big, main thing she'd said: she had kids. "What do you mean, desperate?" He was stalling for time, trying to wrap his mind around the concept of April, not much more than a kid herself, having kids. Plural.

"My kids weren't doing well where we lived before. I want to start over here, where I have some family. This job offered the perfect opportunity."

He wanted to keep being mad, but another feeling was seeping in there: sympathy. "I'm sorry about your dad," he said. "My brother told me."

"Yeah, well. Thanks." She flashed the slightest smile. "Having him gone hurts, but it does make it easier for me to move back home. We were…estranged."

"I'm sorry to hear it," he said automatically, even though he wasn't surprised. Her father had been a hard man, not the best to raise a young girl alone. His own family had come in conflict with her dad, multiple times. It could almost be classified as a feud.

"Mom! Hey, Mom!" A little blonde girl rushed forward and crashed into April, wrapping her arms around her mother's legs. A few seconds later, a blond boy came at a slower pace. April knelt so she could wrap an arm around both children.

Frank stared as facts and assumptions swirled through his mind. When she'd said "kids," he'd assumed she'd meant a couple of toddlers. These were school-aged kids, five or six. She must have had them young.

Like, when she was eighteen.

Like, when he'd dated her, until she'd cheated on him.

The two kids were talking over each

other, trying to tell their mother something they'd seen. It gave Frank the chance to study them.

His cop-mind automatically clicked through the suspects. Who had she cheated with? That summer kid who'd worked in the ice cream shop? He'd been blond. Or had it been Ian Fredrickson, Frank's football friend who'd come home that same summer and palled around with them?

The kids were looking at him now, and April's lips were moving, saying something. Her expression held forced cheerfulness.

He swayed a little and Dozer straightened, moving slightly in front of Frank. He was a brace-and-mobility dog, but the rottweiler breed were guardians and protectors. Apparently, Dozer saw the woman and kids before them as a threat.

Dozer was a smart dog.

The little boy ducked back behind April's legs, peeking out at Frank and Dozer. The girl stood straight and glared right back at Dozer. Bit of the bulldozer in her, too, Frank sensed, and a sudden wave of amusement overtook him. He liked kids. Would probably like these little ones, if they weren't the children of whoever had stolen April from him.

Not that she'd put up any resistance, according to what he'd heard. "It's not going to work," he repeated, looking April in the eyes, "but I'm not heartless. You can stay in the place until you make other plans." Then he frowned. She hadn't been the mooching type before, or he hadn't thought so. But then, he'd never really known her. "A week, I mean. Not months."

She bit her lip and looked from her pickup to the carriage house.

That was when he realized her truck was full of boxes and a few pieces of furniture. The carriage house came furnished, but apparently it was rudimentary. He'd only arrived at the rental last night himself, and hadn't had time to look around.

"I'll help you move your stuff inside,"

he said. "You can't leave it out, even for a few days. The weather will change."

"Thanks, but…" She looked from him to Dozer and back again. "*Can* you help? I was planning to call my cousin…"

He clenched his jaw against what he wanted to say: *I'm still a man, I can lift a box!* It was one reason he worked out like a serious athlete. He had to carry in one arm what most guys could carry in two, so that he could keep one hand on Dozer's harness. He didn't appreciate her questioning his strength, but he shouldn't blame her for it.

It wasn't her fault he had balance issues. He was just mad at the world. That was what this writing project was supposed to address, in addition to making him a bunch of money if LaWanda, his agent, were to be believed.

They were moving things inside, the twins giving him and Dozer a wide berth, when he heard shouts and laughter along with the sound of crunching gravel. Car doors opened and closed.

Dozer gave one sharp bark. His stub of a tail started to wag.

A Yorkie, smaller than Dozer's head, came tearing around the corner toward the carriage house, yapping.

Frank set down the box he was carrying, carefully. "At ease," he said to Dozer.

Dozer dropped, and the little Yorkie ran circles around him. April's daughter shrieked with laughter. Her son tugged at Frank's pant leg. "He could hurt that little dog," he said, sounding worried.

Frank knelt beside the boy. "Dozer and Mork are good friends," he said. "Dozer would never hurt him. Or a kid, either," he added, and the little boy's tense shoulders relaxed a little.

The voices he'd heard came closer and more car doors slammed. Frank looked over at April. "Like it or not," he said, "I think you're about to encounter the whole Wilkins clan."

Chapter Two

❧

Don't panic, April told herself.

Just because Frank's three brothers and their wives and kids were swarming around them, some dressed ridiculously in shorts and flip-flops, with blankets or big puffer coats against the cold...there was no need to panic. Surely they'd leave soon.

After a flurry of awkward greetings, a big jovial argument ensued between Frank and his brothers. Frank was trying to explain that he had a meeting scheduled with April and couldn't join them on whatever they had planned. His brothers and their wives urged him to bring April along on their outing. They reminded him that it was a holiday, that it didn't make sense to work when there was a polar bear plunge happening half a block away at the Holiday Point park.

The fact that Cam and Alec and Fisk, plus Fisk's wife, Lauren, were about to jump into an icy river explained their odd attire.

The twins hung back, pressed to April's side, while the big Wilkins family clustered around Frank. But the mention of polar bears made them both go wide-eyed. "Can we go, Mom?" Evelyn begged. "I want to see polar bears!"

"Me, too," Eli said.

"I don't think there are real polar bears," she said. "We'd better stay here and bring in the boxes from the truck."

The brothers waved aside that objection. They made an assembly line and within ten minutes, all April's boxes were stacked neatly in the house's common living room.

Whether they'd get to unpack them and

stay out the whole six weeks was anyone's guess.

Meanwhile, the wives and kids fell over each other explaining the polar bear plunge. "It's not *real* polar bears," ten-year-old Hector explained.

"But there were polar bear stuffies you could buy last year," Hector's younger brother, JJ, who looked to be about the twins' age, said.

"Can we go?" Evelyn begged.

Eli just looked at her with big, pleading eyes.

It was a way to get them involved in the town and with other kids. She was already nodding agreement when realization hit her like a snowball to the face: all of these kids were her kids' relatives. They were cousins.

As they all started walking the few blocks downtown, she thought hard about the situation. She'd known it intellectually, of course. She knew Frank's brothers a little; his family was notorious in Holiday

Point, and she'd met a couple of them. But she hadn't known they all had kids, nor that they would be close with Frank and spending time around them during this six-week-long job.

She'd been so caught up in her worries about finding work and moving to what felt like a safe haven that she hadn't considered all the ramifications—like how if they moved to Holiday Point permanently, they'd be smack in the middle of a big, tightly connected family.

To be fair to herself, she hadn't known the Wilkinses would be involved in her life at all, because she hadn't known Frank was back in Holiday Point. The last she'd heard, he had moved away and never came back, not even for visits. All of this was so unexpected that her head was spinning.

But as she watched the kids, her heart seemed to swell with longing. It would be so, so good for the twins to grow up surrounded by extended family like this. Even now, Hector was showing Eli how to improve his aim when throwing snow-balls. Eli was smiling and looking excited. Evelyn had taken a little girl named Bonita, who seemed to be the daughter of Frank's brother Fisk, under her wing and was walking slowly, holding the little girl's hand.

The truth had to come out. She *wanted* it to come out. She knew that, instantly.

She needed to tell the whole extended family what was going on, tell them all that the twins were, in fact, their kin. But first, she had to tell Frank.

She'd figured that he'd known she was pregnant, maybe that he'd even told his brothers. But they were introducing themselves and asking questions about the kids as if they'd had no idea.

That must mean Frank didn't know.

She watched him for a few minutes and her conclusion was confirmed: he didn't know. She could tell by the bemused way he dealt with all the kids, nothing special for the twins.

So if it hadn't been because he'd heard she'd been pregnant and wanted to escape his responsibility, then why had he left her without a trace? And if he'd abandoned her once for no apparent reason, would he abandon her and the kids again?

The whole situation was kind of a mess. If they hung out with Frank's brothers and their kids, how would it work to tell them later that they were all, in fact, related? Would the brothers and their wives be angry at her for keeping the secret?

But it wasn't exactly a secret. It was just that she hadn't thought any of the Wilkinses would care.

She took a deep breath and focused on her faith. Even when she was confused or felt that there was nowhere else to turn, God was her mainstay and her support. He would straighten it out, work it for good. He always did.

They walked slowly through town, headed toward the park along with numerous other families, couples and individuals.

April looked at the pretty Victorian houses all in a row, the nicely decorated front porches, the picket fences. She smelled wood smoke from fireplaces and listened to conversations and bursts of laughter.

Eli walked alongside her, holding her hand, taking it all in. Evelyn had run ahead and was chattering rapidly with another girl who looked to be her age. The other little girl pointed, then ran to a woman and started tugging her back toward Evelyn. A moment later, the woman and the two girls came back to walk alongside her and Eli.

"This is our teacher!" The words exploded out of Evelyn's mouth as she approached. She loved being the first to share good news.

"Hi, I'm Olivia Constantine," the woman said, holding out a hand to shake April's. "I saw your kids' names on my roster. So glad I get to meet them ahead of time."

"Me, too," April said, even as she worried inwardly. If the twins liked their new teacher, that would just be another reason they wanted to stay here. Unfortunately, April wasn't sure if she could manage working closely with Frank.

But it would really be good if they liked their teacher. Working with Frank was short-term. Once she found herself and the kids a new, permanent place to live and some kind of work to pay the bills—*if* she found all that—then the twins could be in a good environment. She wouldn't need to be all that close with Frank.

Unless he wanted to share custody...

Oh, man. There were so many angles to this, now that she understood that her mysterious writer-employer was Frank, the father of her children.

Olivia fell into step beside them. "You're going to love first grade," she said to Eli, glancing over at Evelyn to include her, too. "We learn, but we make it fun."

"I love to learn," Evelyn said proudly.

Eli bit his lip. He looked up at Olivia, then away.

"What do you like to do, Eli?" Olivia asked.

He reached out and made a squiggling motion with his hand, then moved closer to April's side.

"Eli likes to draw," Evelyn said. "He's a good drawer."

"That's wonderful," Olivia said. "We do a lot of drawing, and coloring, and even some painting in my class."

Eli didn't say anything, but he smiled and his chin lifted.

"I understand you're doing a tour of the school tomorrow?" Olivia asked April.

"We plan to." Unless the situation went badly downhill.

"I'll be there putting the finishing touches on the classroom in the morning," Olivia said. "Maybe I'll see you then. If not, then I'll see you when class starts back up on Wednesday." She gave the kids a big smile, shook April's hand and jogged back to a tall man, a boy who looked just a bit older than the twins and a reddish dog in a service vest.

As April and the kids walked on with the Wilkins clan, the streets grew more crowded. Every parking place in the lot was taken. Crowds of people stood at the bank of the river, and an announcer called people's names and explained the event's rules. A young man in a jacket that read Lifeguard stood on a flat rock above the water, arms crossed, several life preservers at his side. Close to the river's edge, an ambulance sat at the ready, with two EMTs leaning against it. Of course, that would be a requirement. Jumping into ice-cold water could be extremely detrimental if the wrong person did it.

She wondered, suddenly, whether Frank would do the plunge. She didn't know anything about him and his condition. She'd seen him lean against his service dog, so something must be physically wrong.

"I remember seeing you when we were in school, but I don't think we've ever talked," Kelly, Alec Wilkins's wife, said as she fell into step beside April, her adorable baby on her hip. As April recalled, Kelly had been a popular senior when April was a freshman in high school. "So you're here to help Frank write a book? Is it temporary?"

April nodded, then frowned. "It's just six weeks, but I'm hoping we can stay in Holiday Point if everything works out. I had a good childhood here, even with some... family issues." She never wanted to speak ill of her father. Despite everything, she'd loved him dearly and it had gutted her each time he'd rejected her overtures. "I'd love for my kids to have the same kind of old-fashioned childhood."

Kelly nodded her approval. "That's the reason Alec came back to Holiday Point," she said. "He was a single dad, and he thought this would be better than city life. And it is."

"So...which ones are yours?" April couldn't keep the gaggle of kids straight as they ran and played in the snow. She was thankful her own kids had bright blue jackets and hats, different from anyone else's, so she could keep good track of them.

Kelly pointed out her six-year-old daughter, but then everyone was swept up into the excitement of the crowd. "I have to go make sure Zinnia doesn't jump in after Alec," she said, and hurried off toward the little girl.

The brothers were stripping off coats and all but T-shirts and athletic shorts, and against her will, April felt worried about Frank. She stood on tiptoes to see past others.

Then she saw him and her breath caught.

He took off his coat and shoes and headed toward the riverbank with the others, still wearing jeans. He moved just fine, so his dog wasn't for a limb disability or something like that. He got jostled in the crowd, though, and leaned on his rottweiler.

Seeing him in a short-sleeved T-shirt, April realized that he'd gotten even more muscular than he'd been when she'd known him before.

"Oh, no." Kelly was beside April again. "Frank shouldn't be doing this."

"Especially in jeans," Olivia said from her other side.

April's stomach twisted. She had plenty of issues with Frank, but he was the father of her children. She didn't want to see him hurt.

"The guys should have told him to wear shorts," Kelly said. "Nobody knew he'd try to do the plunge, though. We should stop him."

But it was too late. The host's amplified patter turned into a count, and then a whistle blew and all the participants jumped into the icy river.

The thirty or so people who'd jumped surfaced immediately, sputtering and laughing and shouting. The kids, Eli and Evelyn among them, watched and laughed and squealed, safely away from the river's edge.

April, along with other friends and family members, hurried toward the water and the laughing, emerging participants.

Frank stood and shook water out of his hair, smiling and laughing.

As he and the others came out of the water, Frank's brother Alec walked beside him, watching, not laughing. Frank staggered a little in his wet, heavy jeans, and Alec caught his arm.

Frank pulled away as they reached dry land. In the midst of the crowd, no one who wasn't specifically watching Frank would notice that he was unsteady.

Dozer noticed, though. He pushed his way through the talking, laughing spectators and reached Frank just as the big man started to sway. The dog braced itself right beside him, and Frank caught his harness and managed to avoid falling. The dog gave a little yelp.

With Dozer's help, Frank eased himself

to the ground. He checked the dog's shoulders and body. His face was red, whether because of the cold or embarrassment, she couldn't tell.

Most of the others who'd plunged into the river now had blankets wrapped around them. "We need an extra blanket for Frank," she called to Kelly, and the woman hurried over with a large woolen blanket.

The rest of the kids seemed to be with their parents. No one had noticed Frank's near fall.

Except for Eli, who ran to him, followed closely by Evelyn.

"Are you okay?" Eli asked.

"Is Dozer okay?" Evelyn added.

April hurried over. "Kids, don't—"

"It's fine," Frank said, his breath coming fast, making clouds in the cool air. "He's trained to help me," Frank explained. "I was in an accident in West Virginia a couple of years ago, and I have problems with balance. That's why Dozer wears a harness and sticks close."

"How come he didn't jump in with you?" Evelyn asked.

"Because I told him to stay. He's well trained." Frank rubbed the big dog's head.

As the kids were swept away with their cousins, Frank got to his feet and walked with April, his big frame wrapped in the blanket Kelly had brought him.

She looked up at him. "A better question might be, why did you jump in?"

"Just me being reckless," Frank said. "You should have been informed by my agent that you would be working with someone who has a serious disability. And a tendency to do asinine stuff."

"She mentioned the disability, though she didn't specify what it was. She left out the tendency to take risks."

"Is either thing a problem?" he asked.

"Of course not. Not unless you try to get my kids to do risky stuff."

"I wouldn't. I won't."

She smiled hesitantly, glancing over at him. He wasn't smiling, but he didn't look as upset as he had when he'd initially encountered her. "How about you?" he asked, one eyebrow cocked. "Are you a risk-taker?"

I went out with you when I was eighteen and you were twenty-five. She thought the words, but didn't say them. "Not anymore," she said finally. Her gaze caught his again, got stuck there for a few seconds.

Then they both looked away, and the kids provided April an excuse to walk away. He joined his brothers, who were ribbing him.

But April couldn't stop thinking about that exchange of glances. Nor about how she'd felt, watching Frank.

He was way too appealing, just as he'd been seven years ago. She had to be careful, probably shouldn't stay. He'd abandoned her without warning, and she could never put herself and her kids at risk for that again.

Frank stood next to the big bonfire organized by the polar bear plunge people. He dried off with the towel his brother Alec threw to him, leaning slightly against Dozer's solid body to make sure he stayed upright.

What on earth had he been thinking?

But he knew exactly what had been going through his head. He wasn't going to stand on the riverbank, warm and dry, while his brothers did the fun, foolhardy thing.

Had the fact that April was watching had anything to do with his reckless actions? Probably.

Which just went to show that he was an idiot. He needed to get out of this ridiculous situation with April before it shattered his mind and his composure.

He needed to get rid of her, and her cute kids, too.

"Didn't think you'd participate, man," his brother Fisk said. "You feeling okay?"

"Fine," Frank said. He glared in a way that he hoped would intimidate Fisk and keep him from probing further.

It didn't work. "You know," Fisk said, "risk-taking comes natural to us Wilkinses.

But that doesn't make it the smart thing to do."

Frank didn't snap at Fisk, not when the man had been through so much. He just nodded and kept silent.

"You coming over to Cam and Jodi's?" Fisk asked.

"What's going on there?"

"New Year's Day party, man." Fisk punched him lightly in the arm. "I know somebody told you about it. One of the wives anyway. They wouldn't leave you out."

"I don't always listen," Frank admitted. It had nothing to do with his brain injury. Just him being a guy.

"You can't miss pork and sauerkraut and black-eyed peas." Fisk waved and headed off toward his wife.

"You should come, Uncle Frank," his niece Zinnia said. "I already invited Eli and Evelyn."

Exactly why he shouldn't go.

"Can't we *please, please, please* go?"

Evelyn's high-pitched voice brought his attention to where April knelt in front of her two kids.

"We have things to do at home," she said.

Eli, the little boy, started to cry silently, shoulders shaking, tears rolling down his face. "They have a *dog*," he choked out. "And *cookies*."

If there was one thing Frank couldn't handle, it was a sad, crying kid. He threw the towel he'd borrowed onto his brother's heap and made his way over, Dozer beside him. "Talk to you a minute?" he asked April.

"Um, okay." She stood, put a hand on each twin's shoulder and nodded toward a nearby snowman being built by a couple of the kids. "You may go and help build the snowman for five minutes, and then we'll go."

"To the party?" Evelyn asked, smiling winningly up at her mom.

"You'll find out later," April said, pushing her features into a frown.

"Yay! We can come!" Evelyn ran over to the snowman-builders to announce the good news. Eli frowned, looked from Evelyn to his mother and back again, and then he, too, ran toward the snowman.

"Are you always this strict with them?" he asked, smiling to let her know he was joking.

She rolled her eyes and laughed. "Always. Did you still want to have our meeting, or..."

"Yesss," he said, drawing out the word as he thought about it. "We should meet, but you may as well bring the kids over to my brother's place for an hour or two. It's a free meal."

She raised an eyebrow, her lips pursing a little. "I can afford to feed my kids," she said.

Uh-oh. He hadn't meant to question her ability to provide. "I just meant it's nice not to have to cook. And I'm pretty sure Jodi will have her famous lemon cake."

It was a calculated risk, reminding her

of a bakery item they'd often shared during their relationship. Once he'd learned it was her favorite treat, he'd made sure to get her a piece almost every time they'd gone out for a date.

Would the memory upset her, push her away?

Would that be a bad thing?

Instead of looking put off, her eyes darkened. "I do like lemon cake," she said in that sultry voice that seemed to come to her so naturally.

Frank's breath caught in his throat. He found himself looking deeply into those blue-green eyes.

You're trying to get her to leave, fool, not bait the hook with lemon cake. But he'd already done it. Now he had to deal with what he'd said. "Look, working together isn't an ideal situation and we both know it. Maybe we can get a chance to talk for a few minutes while the kids are occupied at Cam's place."

She studied him as if she were trying to

read his mind, his intentions, his soul. "All right," she said finally. "We can come, provided we try to find a chance to talk about our situation."

Half an hour later, they were at his brother's house. Frank was feeling better—or at least drier—after borrowing a ridiculous pair of plaid flannel pants from his brother.

When he came out in them, Cam and Alec gave identical snorts. "Dress to impress, I always say," Alec said.

"Pretty sure he was trying to make an impression on *someone* when he jumped in that water," Cam said. "You may think nobody noticed, but I saw you. You almost went down afterward."

"Yeah. That was…ill-advised." He went over to stand by the fire. He'd let Dozer out of his harness and the rottweiler was nosing happily at little Mork.

"So, are you really going to work with your ex-girlfriend who broke your heart?" his brother Cam asked.

Frank was about knocked down by the

wave of feelings that question evoked. Images of working with the shiny-haired vixen who'd cheated on him seven years ago made his head spin. But he couldn't ignore the question, not with all his brothers watching and waiting.

"I might," he said with a heavy sigh.

"Doesn't seem wise," Alec said. "Don't you have to control stress?"

"Like jumping into an ice-cold river isn't stress," Cam said with another snort.

"To be fair," Fisk said, "a lot of us need to avoid stress. But that doesn't mean we can't do anything risky. Everyone needs a little excitement in their lives."

Cam nodded. "Especially Wilkinses."

"I'm behind you doing the polar bear plunge," Fisk said, "but let me tell you, working with someone when you feel… *complicated* about them can be tough."

Fisk should know. He'd taken on an assistant last Christmas who'd ended up becoming his wife.

"I probably shouldn't," Frank admitted. "It's hard to imagine it going well."

"But consider," Cam's wife, Jodi, said, coming in with a spatula in her hand and pointing it at Frank. "She's moved here for this job. She gave up her apartment in Chicago, and her kids are enrolled in school."

How had Jodi learned all that in the few short hours since she'd first seen April? "I'm aware," Frank said, feeling uneasy, "but those were decisions she made."

"Based on your agent's promises," Jodi said. A timer went off in the kitchen and she turned away.

With his uncanny sense of where April was—something he'd seemed to redevelop today—Frank saw Jodi take a sidestep to intercept April as she walked through the hallway. The two women spoke, quietly but intensely, and Jodi nodded toward the men. Then there was a shout from the kitchen and Jodi rushed away, clearly needed in the latest cooking emergency.

April straightened her spine and lifted

her chin, and then she walked in. Ignoring his brothers—no easy feat, as there wasn't a one of them under six foot two, two hundred pounds—she stopped in front of Frank. "Ready to talk this through?" she asked.

"Sure." Frank gestured toward the back of the house. "There's a porch back there. It's a little chilly, but we—I mean, you—can watch the kids outside." He wasn't sure what had made him say "we." He wasn't involved with those kids.

Except he felt for them, Eli in particular. Little guy seemed a bit lost.

Cam gave another, barely audible snort. "Make yourselves at home."

"This way," Frank said, stepping to one side to usher her out. He swayed a little and caught himself on the doorjamb, and his face heated. He shouldn't have let Dozer out of harness; the dip in the river had taken a lot out of Frank. But he hated to admit or display his weakness in front of his brothers—and especially in front of April.

They went to the little enclosed porch, and Frank lifted the covers off a couple of chairs. "Sit down," he said. "Want something hot to drink?" It really was cold out here. His breath made clouds in the air.

April shook her head, looking impatient. "I just need to know," she said, "whether you're going to keep me on or not."

"I haven't quite figured that out."

"Well, figure fast."

He frowned at her, raising his eyebrows. He didn't remember her being this unreasonable. "Working together got sprung on me, on both of us, just this morning. Surely you can't expect an answer in less than twenty-four hours."

"I don't expect it, but I *need* it," she said. "I need to know whether to buy groceries. Whether to take the kids for the school tour tomorrow. Should I unpack? Stuff like that might not seem super important to a single individual, but to a mom with two needy kids, it's crucial."

That made sense, but Frank still didn't have an answer for her. So he zeroed in on something that made him curious. "How are they needy?" he asked. "Is something wrong?"

She stretched out her neck from one side to another, raised and lowered her shoulders. She was stressed, for sure. "Our living conditions and the local public school weren't ideal."

Living conditions? He wanted to probe that further, but he had to recognize it wasn't his business.

What Jodi had said flashed into his mind. *She gave up her apartment. The kids are enrolled in school.*

She was watching him, waiting, biting her lip. When he didn't answer, she spoke again. "I do have a contract," she said. "But if it's truly something that won't work—"

"Whoa whoa whoa." He held up a hand to interrupt her. "I always honor a contract." It was a point of pride with him, related to coming from the disreputable, or at least formerly disreputable, Wilkins family.

Speaking of contracts, he also had a book contract with a deadline, and he needed help. He swayed a little and sat down abruptly.

Overwhelmed. Just like his therapist had said, he could track that by increased balance issues. "It's not a decision to make today," he said. "Stay the week. You'll be paid, and you have lodging for your kids. We'll talk more, maybe try it out, and decide at the end of the week." That was more than generous, he felt. It would give him a chance to see if he could keep his distance from this woman who already drew him like a magnet. She was clearly bad for him, but his emotions didn't know that or didn't buy it.

She sat forward in her chair. In this light, her eyes looked turquoise. "No. That's not acceptable. I can't disrupt my kids, make them change schools and homes again, after just a week. And a week, especially if we're working together, doesn't give me enough time to find something else in Holiday Point."

He saw her point, but he didn't like it. He wasn't the type of person to rush into decisions, not the big ones, anyway. That always got him in trouble.

"I either stay here for the whole six weeks and complete the contract, or I leave tonight," she said. "You need to decide. Now."

She was giving him an ultimatum. Which meant he had to come up with an answer. Immediately.

Chapter Three

April couldn't believe she'd just given Frank an ultimatum.

It was a big risk. He didn't like being pushed into a corner. She remembered an immature "go with me to this party or I'll dump you" argument they'd had when they dated years ago. When she'd made her demand then, he'd just lifted an eyebrow and smiled. "You really want to give up this thing we've got going for a high school party?" he'd asked.

Of course, she'd given in and sat on his lap and kissed him, and then he'd come to the party anyway, just to be nice.

Which had made her fall a little more in love with him.

Now the stakes were so much higher. Now she had a good reason for an ultimatum: she had to take care of her kids.

If he would bend his usual way of doing things to accommodate them, and her, it would be the evidence she needed that he was truly a good person. She'd tell him the truth about the kids and invite him into their lives.

Not just tell Frank. Tell all of them, she thought, listening to the lively conversation and music and laughter in the house behind them. Visible through the doorway that led inside, she could see Eli sitting cross-legged on the floor playing with Dozer and the little Yorkie Mork, a girl of his age beside him. A cousin, though she couldn't quite remember her name or to whom she belonged.

Outside, Evelyn was intently focused on building a snow fort with several of the other kids. Snow had started to fall again, just lightly.

She wanted this for her kids. Not as outsiders, but as members of the family. She wanted them to know they legitimately belonged to the Wilkins clan. It would be so, so good for both of them.

When she looked at Frank again, he was studying her, his head tilted a little to one side.

It all depended on him, though. Yes, he and his brothers seemed great—which was pretty amazing given what they'd come from—but Frank had been through a lot and he had a temper. If he couldn't even handle working with her for six weeks, then there was no way he'd embrace and accept her kids.

His kids. Their kids.

"There's a problem," he said finally.

"With what?"

"Our history," he said.

If only you knew. "Do we really want to

go there?" She *did* want to tell him about the kids, eventually. Just not now.

He studied her without saying anything.

She looked away, her face heating. Outside, kids shouted as someone lobbed the first volley in what would undoubtedly be an epic snow battle.

"April."

Hearing him say her name like that made her breath catch for some reason she didn't understand. "What?"

"I don't know if it's possible for us to work together comfortably. We can say we're going to leave the past in the past, but...sometimes feelings come up whether we want them to or not."

Was he talking about his anger toward her? Guilt about ghosting her? Or was it something else, related to that awareness she'd seen a couple of times in his eyes today?

Feeling the rapid thump of her own heartbeat, she knew there was some kind of awareness in her expression, too.

But she needed to focus. She was a mom, and that came first. "I'm gonna suggest that we get through this project and make it a success before we dig into any past territory that might have land mines."

He looked away, out the window, arms crossed over his chest. She had the feeling he wasn't seeing the kids at play.

If he bit, if he agreed to let her stay and do the project with him, could they really avoid their history?

It would be best to try. The truth might cause him to dump her as a writing partner, which would mean she was out of a job and the kids were out of a home. She didn't have an alternative lined up, not yet, and what she was really angling for was stability for Evelyn and Eli.

He looked back at her and nodded. "I need your help and I want to follow through with the contract. So all right. You can stay. Get the kids settled in school, and we'll work hard to get the book done. And then," he said with something she couldn't quite read in his eyes, "and then, we'll see if there's anything we need to discuss about the past."

"Thank you!" Relief washed over her. There was some kind of happy excitement, too, that had nothing to do with the kids. It had to do with Frank. Being near him. Just like before, all he had to do was look at her and she'd melt.

But she was going to ignore that. She and the kids were safe and settled for six weeks. That was what mattered.

She'd use any free time she had to look for another job and a place to live when this short-term contract was over. Once that was all settled, once her paycheck for this job was safely in the bank, then she'd tell him the truth.

As late-morning sunlight filtered into the room he'd claimed as a study, Frank sat waiting for a scheduled call from his agent. He was kicking himself for yesterday's conversation with April. Why had he said she and the kids could stay?

Beside him, Dozer slept directly on the wooden floor, a few feet away from the expensive dog bed Frank's brothers had bought the dog as a Christmas gift.

Or rather, their wives had bought it. He and his brothers had rarely had it together enough to buy each other Christmas gifts, let alone spend money on each other's pets. As each of his brothers had married, observances of holidays had gone up a few levels.

Take yesterday's gathering. Even if he and his brothers had wanted to do a polar bear plunge in years past, they'd have done it and gone home or to a tavern. Bring women into the picture, and all of a sudden there were pretty decorated tables and great smells coming from the kitchen, the sound of happy laughter even though there was no alcohol in sight.

Yes, his brothers had done well for themselves. Chosen good women, settled down, started families of their own.

He was the only one still single.

The buzz of his phone offered a distraction, and he hit the speaker and heard his agent's voice. "Hey, good-lookin,'" she said, shamelessly Southern. "I'm waiting for a thank-you bouquet."

"For what? And hello to you, too. Happy New Year." Frank sat back in his desk chair, his shoulders loosening. He and La-Wanda had met at a writer's conference a year ago. He'd been a mess, trying to hawk his book proposal, figure out his ever-evolving disability and get used to working with Dozer all at the same time. LaWanda had been starting a second career as a literary agent after years as a public school English teacher. Her long white braids and faded jeans and easy laugh had set her apart from the other driven publishing-industry professionals at the conference. They'd bonded as outsiders, and

Frank had never regretted his decision to work with her.

Maybe until now, because he was pretty sure he knew what she was talking about.

"You should be bowing down to thank me for finding April Collins," LaWanda went on. "Isn't she a treasure? I hope you showed her a little bit of that Wilkins charm, or were you too cranky about that deadline you're facing?"

"Neither, and I'll meet the deadline." He had to. Meeting deadlines and honoring commitments were how he showed the world he wasn't like his dad.

"Good. I was thrilled when she applied to co-write with you. She's the real deal, has got the skills, *and* she's willing to spend six weeks in that…*hamlet* you seem to want to settle down in."

"Yeah." He debated whether to tell La-Wanda that her perfect solution wasn't perfect.

Of course, she guessed something was wrong. She hadn't raised two boys without learning how to read what was beneath the surface. "What is it, Frank?"

Busted. "There's a history. Between me and April."

"Aaahhhh." She was quiet a moment. "And we didn't publicize your name, and... well, I guess it *is* a small community. Can you work with her?" She sounded worried. This was the biggest contract she'd negotiated so far, and if he didn't hold up his end of it, her name in the industry would be tarnished and her income cut.

Not to mention his own income. Between his veterans' benefits and his police disability pay, he was okay for now. But he needed to start bringing money in. The advance from this book was supposed to bridge the gap until he found something else.

LaWanda and his editors seemed to think this project had the potential to go big. Frank just wanted to get by, maybe even a little bit ahead.

Ahead enough to head a family, maybe.

He stood and walked over to the window. April and the twins were down by the river, all wearing boots against the slushy snow. April was laughing at something Eli had said.

He swallowed. "I can work with her."

"You'd best keep it professional until the job's over," she said. "Can you do that? She's a real nice girl. Hardworking." There was a hint of the protective mother bear in LaWanda's voice.

It was enough to tear Frank's eyes away from April. "Of course. There's no chance of anything between us now."

"Uh-huh. Well, I just wanted to touch base about April and the project," she said, and they ended the call.

The call had done what it should; it had focused him. Reminded him that in addition to the publishing company, LaWanda was depending on his fulfilling the contract.

And there was the bigger picture, getting the story out there, showing people the complexity of the situation. He owed it to his brother and sister officers and the people of the drug-ridden town where it had all gone down.

He had to get over himself and do his job. Any out-of-place feelings that might come up, he could squelch. He was a pro at squelching feelings. A cop had to be.

Downstairs, a door opened, then another. Whoever was down there was trying to be quiet. He glanced out the window again and saw that April was talking to a neighbor. In the neighbor's yard, several kids were building a snowman.

April was making friends with the neighbors already. Of course she was. She'd always been easy with people, good at connecting with them. That would be great for her kids.

Another noise downstairs. He didn't have a weapon, but he was pretty confident he could handle himself in a confrontation. Plus, Dozer hadn't barked.

He made his way down and followed the sounds to the pantry.

Evelyn sat on her knees in front of a cabinet, an open bag of cookies in her hand. She was stuffing them into her mouth.

"Hey," he said quietly, not wanting to scare her.

She jolted and jammed the box back into the cupboard just as April came through the back door, looking flushed and tense, with Eli behind her. "Have you seen Evelyn?"

He glanced behind him. Evelyn was brushing crumbs off her shirt, but her chocolaty mouth was going to give her away. He pulled a handkerchief from his pocket and tossed it to her. "She's fine," he said, strolling out into their shared kitchen. "She just needed a snack." He didn't want to rat Evelyn out on gorging, but he figured her mom should know she'd had something to eat.

April threw up her hands. "Evelyn! If you need a snack, you ask me." She toed her boots off, then bent and helped Eli take his off. "And look, you got mud on the floor. I'll have to clean that, you know."

Evelyn came up beside him and gave him back his handkerchief. He pointed to a spot on his own cheek to indicate she'd missed a smudge of chocolate, and she backhanded it away. Then she slipped a hand into his.

All Frank's breath whooshed out of him. The trust in that simple gesture pushed at his heart, hard.

April saw it and her eyebrows shot up.

Then Evelyn dropped his hand, ran to her mother and leaned against her leg, clutching it. "I ate a bunch of cookies, his cookies." She pointed at Frank. "I was hungry and we never had those before."

April rolled her eyes and stroked Evelyn's hair. "You've had plenty of cookies in your life," she said. "You need to apologize to Mr. Wilkins. And you'll need to do an extra chore tonight."

Evelyn peeked out at him. "I'm sorry, Mr. Wilkins." She gave him a sweet smile.

His heart melted. "It's okay. I'm glad to share. Just ask first."

"Did you leave a mess?" April asked.

Evelyn gave a slow nod.

"Get a paper towel and clean it up the best you can."

"I'll help," Eli said. With the ease of experience, he ran to the counter and dropped to all fours. Evelyn climbed on his back and grabbed a wad of paper towels. They did the same routine by the sink, wetting a couple of the towels, and then both of them raced into the pantry.

Her kids. They were a little smaller than was average for their age, but they were definitely resourceful. "I'm sorry," April said to Frank. "I'll replace the cookies."

"It's not a problem," he said. "I shouldn't be eating chocolate-frosted dino cookies anyway."

"You *like* those?"

He nodded. "Love 'em."

She laughed and shook her head. "Terrible taste. I really am sorry."

Concern pushed him to take the conversation a little further. "I've seen that kind of eating behavior in my police work. Did you go through some tough times?"

She looked confused. "We've never had a lot, but we've been fine. Why?"

"Sometimes when kids go through a stage of not having enough to eat, they'll binge when they get the chance."

April's face flushed red. "My children always had enough to eat. We've had to make use of food pantries at times, but we...well, they, at least, have never gone hungry."

He caught the shift, and it gave him another way to look at her slender, youthful build. He was guessing she'd sacrificed her own dinner to feed her kids and gone to bed hungry herself.

"Of course," she said, smiling up at him, "we *did* have a shortage of frosted dino cookies. In that way, they've been deprived."

"Poor things."

"Can I make it up to you by fixing us all some lunch? Or better yet, you could join us for dinner after we get our afternoon's work done. Then it'll be something actually cooked, not just sandwiches."

Frank needed to keep it professional, and he needed to suppress his desire to wrap this beautiful, smiling young mother in his arms. He should get his meals on his own, as he'd planned.

But he was hungry. Not to mention that he wasn't a very good cook, and wasn't looking forward to eating one of the frozen meals he'd stocked. "Thank you. I'd appreciate some dinner."

Chapter Four

April had planned to allow the kids a rare afternoon of TV, but it turned out that the next-door neighbor's kids wanted them to come over. Surprisingly, even Eli wanted to go. That left April free to get started on her work with Frank.

She sat in their shared office reading the notes he'd given her, and an hour or so later he came in, hair damp, face ruddy.

"Sorry I'm late," he said. "Had to fit in my workout. Doctor's orders."

A surge of…something came over April. He was good looking, even more so than when she'd known him before. His workouts were definitely effective.

More than that, he was a real-life, genuine hero. Every page she'd just been reading, his documentation of events leading up to the takedown of a pair of major drug traffickers, showed it. At least if you could read between the lines. Rather than bragging, Frank downplayed his role.

He was an appealing man. She just had to remember that he'd abandoned her before without warning. For her own sake, for her kids' sake, she had to keep him at arm's length.

She cleared her throat. "Glad you got your workout in. I've had plenty to do, going over your notes." She pointed at the stack of mismatched papers in front of her.

He winced. "They're a mess."

"They are," she agreed. "But, wow, I'm impressed with the role you played."

He waved her comment away. "Any operation like that takes a team. I want to be sure to portray that, not inflate my own role."

She liked that about him. So many ac-

complished men were a little full of themselves. Frank wasn't.

She folded her hands together, elbows
resting on the desk, and smiled up at him.
"Noted. But you shouldn't deflate your
role, either."

"We'll seek out a balance," he said, smiling back.

Their eyes met for a little too long. The
only sound was the click of Dozer's toe-
nails as he padded in, out of harness.

The slight distraction snapped April
back into her thinking brain. "We need to
get organized," she said, going for a brisk,
businesslike tone. "I've got these roughly
sorted by chronology, but we need to figure out subcategories." She showed him
what she meant and they worked together
for an hour, quiet except for a few quick
questions and replies.

The desk got overfull of little stacks. "I
saw a long table in the garage," he said,
and started off to get it. When he heard

her following, he turned. "You don't have to come. I can get this myself."

"I'm sure, but why would you when there's someone willing to help?"

He lifted an eyebrow like she'd said something profound. "Good point. It's over here."

They carried the table back and set it up. "It's crowded in here now," April said, looking around, hands on hips. "But it's only until we get the notes sorted and entered into the computer."

"Makes sense."

Half an hour later, her cut-and-paste organizational method had created order. "You just keep making notes, either on paper or on your laptop, but try to keep them in these categories. I'll put it all together and then you can edit. If we get this much done every day, we'll meet your deadline."

"You're good at this." Surprise and admiration were in his tone. "How'd you get so organized?"

Hearing the praise felt good. "You have to get organized when you're a single mom of twins, especially now that they're in school. Two of everything, including a lot of paperwork. And don't even get me started on managing a birthday party for two on a budget." She frowned. "Speaking of which, that's coming up in March. I'll have to start making a plan just as soon as we finish our project."

"They'll be six?"

"Seven," she said.

He started to nod and then frowned, looking thoughtful.

He's doing the math in his head.

Uh-oh. If he was counting backward from March, he was about to figure out that he was the twins' father. Her whole body seemed to freeze, except for her pounding heart.

The sound of the kids bursting through the kitchen door cut off any chance of discussing those numbers. April knew it was cowardly, but she was glad. She wasn't ready to tell him the whole truth, not when they were just getting started on their project.

Not when these sweaty, adorable kids depended on her—and only her—to put food on the table for dinner.

And then she realized with a sinking feeling that Frank was coming to dinner. Tonight. With even a couple minutes of math and calendars, he'd guess the truth.

Wouldn't he? How could he not?

Frank stayed in his office as long as he could, looking at two dozen stacks of papers, paper-clipped together and labeled with Post-it notes.

How could April be such a talented individual and so sweet on the surface, and yet be false, disloyal, a cheater?

His father was the one who'd broken it to him, and he'd conveyed a few too many details about her escapades. But for the past five years, Frank had been able to push it all out of his mind. The betrayal had affected him; no doubt it was the reason he didn't do serious relationships. But as for actual memories and emotional pain, he'd pretty much suppressed it all.

"Dinner in ten minutes," Evelyn recited from the doorway.

"I'll be there," he assured the little girl. She smiled and spun back toward the kitchen, and Frank stared gloomily after her.

The problem was those kids. They were obviously the direct result of April cheating on him, and his mind kept working over who it might have been.

If they'd been full term, then the conception must have happened toward the beginning of his relationship with April, which had lasted only three months. She must have been intimate with someone else early on. But twins often weren't full term. If it was later…

Stop. He needed to stop thinking. Thinking could destroy you.

He pulled in a deep breath. Deliberately

he focused on the warmth of the gas fireplace, the bookshelves that lined one wall, one of them stocked with those old-fashioned plain volumes, the rest holding little decorations—ships and a clock and a geode rock, its glittering insides sparkling in the sun. The turquoise color was almost exactly the same as April's eyes...

Stop. Breathe.

That, along with focusing on the senses, had been a suggestion from the therapist he'd worked with after his injury. Frank wasn't one to sit and meditate, but he did experience peaceful focus in nature, and in church, on a regular basis. In those beautiful, spiritual places, he could turn off his racing thoughts and be in the moment.

When he let his thoughts run away with him, they often ran to the past. Thinking about the big shoot-out gone wrong that had ended his police career, or a few other things he'd seen and done in his military and police years, could send him into full-on panic mode. Adrenaline rushing, heart pounding, muscles tensed, ready to fight.

Which wasn't that different from how he was feeling now, in the presence of April and her two freakily adorable kids who were the result of her cheating on him.

Could they be his? They'd gone too far, once. Of course he'd used protection, but there was a slim chance it had failed. She'd said it was her first time and she'd cried afterward, and he'd promised not to let it happen again. He'd kept the promise, too.

Even though he hadn't been a Christian at the time, he'd had a conscience. He'd felt terrible about their onetime lack of restraint. He was older and should have taken responsibility for keeping them on the right track. His guilt had pushed him further toward thoughts of marriage, in fact.

But given what his dad had told him, the tears had been crocodile tears, the "first time" statement a lie. April had been with at least two other guys—repeatedly. The odds of his being the father were very much not in his favor. And surely he'd have heard if they were his. Surely she'd have told him.

He didn't want to go into their shared kitchen and eat a meal with April and her kids. He'd rather just grab a sandwich and head up to his private quarters. But he'd said he would, so he would. Breaking promises and disappointing kids were things his father did, not him. He forced himself to walk in.

She'd made some kind of Beefaroni thing, more noodles than beef, and she didn't apologize for it. Beefaroni and rolls and salad, with cookies from the cookie jar promised to those who finished their dinners. It was the kind of humble family dinner he'd shared lately with his brothers.

April would fit right in here in Holiday Point.

He didn't want to say that, though, because he didn't want her to stay. He absolutely didn't. He wanted to nudge her out of here before she wrapped herself around his heart again.

"Mr. Frank, you sit here," Evelyn said. "But don't sit down yet. We hafta pray."

April smiled an apology as she brought in glasses of water. "Evelyn, thank you, but that's enough. Mr. Frank can figure out what to do." She turned to him. "What can I get you to drink, besides water? You've seen what we have. Tea, coffee, lemonade…"

He'd been going to stick to water. "Lemonade sounds good," he heard himself saying to his own surprise. He hadn't had a glass of lemonade in years.

"Me and Eli want lemonade," Evelyn said, and Eli nodded once. He didn't look as peppy as his sister, Frank noticed.

April brought in glasses and a pitcher of lemonade. They prayed, standing behind their chairs, and then sat down and dug in.

Except for Eli, who ran his fork through his food in aimless patterns on his plate.

"You're not hungry, buddy?" April asked,

putting down her fork and studying him with concern.

Eli shook his head, staring down at the table.

"He doesn't want to go to school," Evelyn said between bites. She spoke with the authority of a kid who'd been interpreting her brother's emotions for years.

Frank didn't want to care about Eli, given that he and his sister were likely the product of April's unfaithfulness to him. Deliberately, he took another roll and buttered it, ignoring the tug at his own heart.

"You need to eat three bites," April said to Eli. "We have cookies for dessert. Chocolate chip, your favorite."

Eli's eyes brightened for a few seconds. Then he looked back down at his plate. He didn't eat the requisite three bites.

Evelyn and April looked at him with matching wrinkled frowns and wrinkled foreheads. Once dinner ended, the cookies didn't come out. April appeared to be the kind of mom who stuck to her threats and promises.

Thinking of his own childhood, Frank was stunned that Evelyn didn't demand cookies. After all, *she* had cleaned her plate.

His own siblings would have been lording it over the one who didn't get any dessert. Not that any of them would've left food on their plates. They'd never gone hungry, but home-cooked meals hadn't been a regular feature of their childhood. Nor had actual thought-out discipline, come to think of it. It was more likely he or one of his brothers would get a quick backhand for poor behavior or for making their dad angry.

Looking at the little bundle of misery that was Eli, Frank gave up on his effort not to care. He couldn't leave the dinner table without trying to help. "Did you meet my brother Fisk?" he asked April, making sure that Eli was listening.

She nodded. "The one with the doodle?"

"Nemo," Evelyn offered helpfully. "That's the doodle's name. Nemo, like in the movie."

"That's right," Frank said. "Anyway, Fisk hated school when he was little."

Eli looked up quickly, but didn't say anything.

"How come he hated it?" Evelyn asked.

"What did your parents do?" April asked at the same time.

"He hated it because it was hard for him. He didn't see things the way other kids did, nor the way the teacher did. He fell behind, got in trouble some." Better not lean on that aspect very heavily in front of the twins. "My parents were...busy with things. They didn't much notice how he was doing."

"But he ended up graduating, didn't he?"

"He did. What helped was a good teacher. Someone who saw him for who he was and who listened to him."

"Good teachers are important," April agreed. She plunged a pan into hot soapy water.

"Once his teacher saw how smart he was, he kind of came into his own. Excelled in art."

"Eli likes art!" Evelyn sounded amazed at the similarity.

"Yes, he does," April said. "And Mrs. Constantine seems like the kind of teacher to appreciate all different kinds of students. I know you'll get to do art in her class." She squeezed Eli's shoulder and smiled at Frank. *Thank you*, she mouthed to him.

"It was too loud at my old school," Eli said quietly. "Some kids didn't follow the rules."

"Understaffed city school," April explained quickly. "Their classroom was right next to one for kids with big behavioral problems. It could get...rough."

"School here will be different," Frank said. "From what I've heard, kids are pretty respectful."

"I like that," Eli said quietly.

"Follow the rules and just be yourself. You'll do well, just like my brother Fisk did." Frank stood. "I should get over to my side of the house. A few things to catch up on."

"Thanks for coming, Frank." April sounded like she meant it. He noticed the tiny dimple in her cheek, which she hadn't displayed much until now. He remembered it from before, though. He'd thought it was cute then, and he still did.

Warmth shot through him at her lingering, grateful smile. He'd done something to help her out, however small. That felt good.

He'd tried to make this dinner brief and businesslike, but due to Eli, he hadn't been able to. As a result, the magnetic pull he felt toward April had increased.

Working together was going to be even harder than he'd expected.

Chapter Five

April did a creditable job of holding it together the next day, her first full day of work with Frank.

Or so she thought at first. They'd continued organizing ideas and hammering out an outline for the book. But in the middle of the afternoon, he suggested they stop for a coffee break. As he made coffee in an old drip pot, she pulled creamer from the fridge and a bag of cookies from the cupboard.

They'd worked together well, but she couldn't stop worrying about Eli. He'd managed to hold back tears this morning, but the fact that he could do that had nearly broken her heart. His time in the tough school had hammered at his sensitive soul. He'd learned to close himself off in a way that wasn't healthy for a first-grader.

"You seem distracted," Frank said as he took the cookies from her hand and set them on the table, then went for plates. He served them both coffee and sat down, and only then did she pull out her own chair and sink into it.

"I'm sorry. You're right, but I'll work on focusing better."

"That's not what I meant. Your work is great. I'm sympathizing as a friend." He took a sip of coffee, grimaced and added creamer. "Worried about the kids?"

"I am. Eli was so shut down when I left. Even Evelyn was concerned about him, which also isn't good. I want her to be able to make her own friends without worrying about her brother."

"Has he always been uncomfortable in school?" Frank opened the bag of cookies and pulled a small mountain of them onto his plate.

She took two and set them down without taking a bite. "He went off to kindergarten excited, like most kids. But he was in a rough classroom. The regular teacher left and there was a series of substitutes, and it was pretty chaotic."

"Was he in a classroom with Evelyn?"

She shook her head. "They wouldn't allow it, and unfortunately, I didn't realize I could fight the policy. He got bullied. I worked with the teacher, but when the subs started cycling through, I couldn't do much to help him."

"Except move?" he asked, eyebrows raised.

"Right. But I'm really sorry my distraction was obvious. It's important to me that we make a success of this project."

He waved a hand. "You're doing fine. We're ahead of where I thought we would be." He sipped coffee. "Boys face some challenges growing up, I think. Challenges that are different from what girls face."

"I guess so. The whole toxic masculinity thing."

He tilted his head, one corner of his mouth lifting. "Yeah, that. I've seen it from all angles, given my line of work and my family."

"My dad definitely struggled with a case of it." An image of her dad in uniform, coming home from a long day of police work, tugged at her heart.

"Mine as well," Frank said, "although from a completely different angle. Guess that's why they were always butting heads."

"That's a nice way of putting it. I worried about actual violence breaking out." She'd worried about it more than Frank could ever imagine. It was what had kept her from revealing that he was the father of her kids, to the town in general and to her father in particular. "I don't want Eli to get drawn into that, but I also don't want him to be bullied."

And then she sucked in a breath. Frank was Eli's father. She was talking to Eli's father about him. "I should head out to get them in a little bit."

"Want me to walk with you?" he asked unexpectedly.

She stared at him. "Why? I mean, you can, but…"

"I can sit with them outside the school or watch them play on the playground while you speak with the teacher a little, ease your mind, find out her perspective."

"You'd do that?"

"Sure. I need to get out of the house."

And you're a kind man. "That would be wonderful. I'll text her and see if she has a minute to chat."

As she did that, he cleared away their coffee things and walked back to the office.

She watched him, bemused. He was a good partner in ways she'd never have expected. She'd known he was masculine and attractive, but not that he was sensitive to other people's needs and willing to go out of his way to help them.

He'd matured, gained wisdom, and it just made the whole package more appealing. It suggested that, when she did reveal the truth about him being the twins' father, he would take responsibility and do a good job with co-parenting.

But she had to remember that she could never, ever get together with Frank, no matter how attracted to him she felt. He'd abandoned her once before with no warning, and he could easily do it again, when it would affect more than just her. It would affect the kids as well.

At four o'clock, April sat down in the twins' classroom, empty now except for Olivia, their new teacher. "Thank you so much for meeting with me," she said. "I won't take too much of your time."

"It's not a problem," Olivia said. "Do you have someone watching the kids after school?"

"They're outside with Frank." April half raised herself out of her seat. Frank stood talking with another man while Evelyn and Eli ran toward the playground, so that was fine. She sat back down.

"Sounds good." Olivia raised an eyebrow and then seemed to school her features into neutrality.

That made April realize how Frank's care of her kids could be misinterpreted. "He was nice enough to offer, and I really wanted to talk to you." Her face felt hot.

"That's great! I'm sure you're wondering how they did in school. And as you might guess, Evelyn got along very well. She seems like a natural leader."

April laughed. "Translation—she's bossy."

"Not in a bad way. She's going to do just fine."

"What about Eli?"

"He'll be fine, too, but it may take a little time." Olivia frowned. "He was looking out the window, upset, and another little boy came over. I think all Roman meant to do was comfort him, but Eli told him to go away and Roman was the one who ended up crying."

"Oh, no. Was Eli rough at all?"

Olivia shook her head. "No, and it's not a problem. Social skills are a big part of what kids learn in the early grades. Little incidents like that give us the chance to talk about manners and kindness."

Great, her kid was an object lesson of how not to act.

Olivia seemed to read her mind. "Half the class had some kind of rough moment today. The first day back from Christmas break is hard. Your kids are both going to be fine, and I'm excited to work with them."

"Thank you so much." April stood to leave, feeling a little better.

Olivia stood, too. "Maybe you'd want to get involved with the class," she suggested. "We have a small team of parent helpers, and one just quit. They're starting to plan the Valentine's party, and I know they could use some help."

"Oh, fun. I'd love to. I mean, I'll have limited time until my project with Frank is done, but I can play a role."

"I'll let the group know." Olivia held up a hand. "Fair warning, the one woman quit because the lead mom can be, well, a little hard to work with. But I'm sure you'll do fine."

"Right. Of course." *This should be interesting.*

Frank had a surprisingly good time watching the kids outside the school. Like most six-year-olds, they were easily entertained: by an icicle hanging from the roof of the building, by rolling a big snowball, and most of all by Dozer, whom Frank let out of harness so he could run and play with them.

He hoped April wasn't the kind of mom to worry about them getting dirty, because between the melting snow and the mud, these clothes would need to go into the wash right away.

Evelyn was clearly the boss, which could be a problem. Not because she was the girl, but because all kids needed to follow orders as well as give them. She was a little general, and he could imagine it causing her a little conflict along the way.

She was whip-smart and cute, though, and it might just be that she'd use her powers for good. She'd make a fine student body president in a few years.

Eli reminded Frank of his brother Fisk. He seemed like a gentle soul. When he knelt to study a patch of ice that was sparkling in the sun, his face conveyed awe and an artistic determination to re-create the beauty in some form. He pulled a grubby piece of paper out of his pocket and started sketching.

But when another little boy came over, Eli didn't just hide his work; he ripped it up and threw it into the trash can, then challenged the kid to a snowball fight. And proceeded to make an icy snowball that could have knocked someone out, if both Frank and Evelyn hadn't rushed over to stop him.

Eli seemed to see the world differently, as most artists did, but in a boy, that could be tough to manage. Frank would hate to see Eli make the same kinds of mistakes Fisk had made.

After all three kids were settled building a snowman—a better use for their excess energy—Frank backed off to let them play. A minute later, April came out.

"How'd it go?" she asked. "Thanks so much for watching them."

"No real problems." He nodded at the kids. "Maybe we should let them play a few minutes. That little boy and Eli nearly got into it, but they seem to be making friends now."

She bit her lip, watching the children. "I worry so much about him. About both of them, really."

"Is their father involved?" As soon as

he'd asked the question, he regretted it. The last thing he wanted to hear about was their father, the person April had cheated with.

She must have been thinking the same, because her face flushed. "No," she said quietly. "At this point, he's not involved."

Frank tried to backpedal. "I'm just asking because of that whole toxic masculinity thing," he said. "Having a male role model could help, maybe. If he were a good one."

She swallowed hard. It almost looked like she was going to cry.

He hadn't meant to upset her like that. He tried to get the conversation back onto less-charged ground. "Like I mentioned earlier, my dad and my brothers had some trouble with that. Always had to act tough. Our dad would just as soon hit you as look at you."

"I remember," she said dryly.

Of course she did. Her father, the police

chief; his father, the town drunk. Yeah. You couldn't get much more opposite.

"How did you boys turn out so well, given the start you had?" She was looking at him with real curiosity and interest.

"The military and sports," he said. "We all learned discipline that way."

"I've thought about getting Eli involved in sports. Both kids, really. Is that a possibility around here? There didn't used to be youth sports for the little ones, as I remember."

"Soccer or T-ball," he said, thinking about his nieces and nephews who were the same age as her kids. "And it's a good idea. You can talk to my brothers about any other opportunities there might be for them during the winter."

"Thanks, I will." She smiled at him. "For now, I think it's time we got these little rascals home and cleaned up and fed."

"I can…" He broke off. He was sliding too easily into acting like a domestic partner. He'd almost offered to cook dinner while she bathed the kids, but was that really his job? "I'll be going out tonight," he improvised quickly. "So you'll have the place to yourself."

And he'd have a chance to cool off and stop acting like Mr. Family Man to a woman who'd already broken his heart once and her way-too-adorable kids.

Chapter Six

❧

On Friday after school, April and the kids walked into the Holiday Point library. A big sign read Crafternoon and an arrow on it pointed them toward the children's department.

They'd gotten through the first week. Eli wasn't any happier with school now than he'd been on their first day, but as he spotted all the craft supplies, his eyes lit up and a shy smile crossed his face.

April's tight shoulders relaxed. Coming here had been Eli's idea, after his teacher had announced the activity to the class. It looked like the kind of thing he'd love.

The children's librarian welcomed everyone in and shepherded them to seats at a couple of tables. Evelyn saw a girl from school and started chatting away at her usual rapid pace. Eli reached for a sheet of paper at the same time another boy did. He smiled at the other boy and let him have the paper. Good. His social skills were already improving.

"April?"

Although she hadn't heard that voice for at least six years, she recognized it immediately. "Nadine! I've been planning to call you!" She hugged her cousin and then stepped back and studied her.

Nadine wore a library employee lanyard with a name tag that read Circulation and Reference. Dressed in black slacks and a blue sweater, her red hair in a ponytail—no makeup—she looked almost exactly the same as she had when they were growing up. Nadine was a year younger than April, but they'd always loved playing together.

"Are you back in town for a while?" Nadine asked.

"I hope so." April explained the job with Frank. "Afterward, I'm hoping to find a place to live and a longer-term job."

"The library can help with that, you know." Nadine gestured toward a bank of computers in the adult section. "We have all kinds of job databases. And people put up old-fashioned paper notices, both for jobs and rentals, on our bulletin board just inside the front door."

"That'll be great! But how are you?"

Nadine shrugged. "Hanging in there. Which ones are the twins?"

April pointed them out, noting that Nadine hadn't said much about her own situation. She'd heard that Nadine had had difficulties, but it was pretty clear she didn't want to talk about it, not here anyway.

Nadine was watching Eli and the little boy next to him. "I'm glad to see that Eli's befriending Thomas. He's homeschooled, and new in town, and it would be nice to see him make some friends."

April tilted her head to one side. "Are you a children's librarian?"

"No. In fact, I'm not a real librarian, just an aide. But we all wear a lot of hats in a small library like this. I've worked a bit with Thomas and his dad."

Nadine was called away to the circulation desk, and after a quick exchange of phone numbers and an agreement to get together soon, she left. April sank into one of the big comfortable chairs in the entryway between the children's and adults' areas, welcoming the chance to sit and think.

Working with Frank was going well. He'd said he was pleased with their progress, and April was, too. The more she learned about his story, the more she wanted to portray it clearly and well. Frank wouldn't admit it, but he was a true hero and had brought down a drug kingpin at the expense of his own health.

Just for a moment, she let herself think

about the times their eyes had met and lingered longer than a boss-employee relationship should merit. And also about the times they'd laughed together, at Dozer's antics or the kids'.

He'd always been an interesting man, but he'd matured into something like wisdom. He wasn't trying to achieve great heights with this book; he just wanted to get the story out. He was exploring job possibilities, too, and April had seen the pain in his eyes when he'd talked about not being able to do police work anymore—pain, but not bitterness. He wasn't one of those people who let a disability define them. He was determined to overcome his vestibular issues and did daily exercises for them, as well as keeping his body in great shape through healthy eating and workouts at a local gym, from which he came home dripping with sweat.

A couple of other mothers were chatting at the edge of the room, and eventually one of them came over. "April Collins! Is that you?"

"Shelby," April said with an internal sigh. Shelby Cooper had been a mean girl back in school, but maybe she'd changed.

"I heard you're living with Frank Wilkins," Shelby said. "Are those his kids?"

All the breath whooshed out of April's lungs. "Uh, uh, what?"

"Are your twins his? They look like him."

"Do they?" she asked, trying to think.

Shelby eyed her shrewdly. "Keeping it to yourself, are you? You know, it's a small town, and word is going to get out sooner or later. Probably sooner."

"I don't know what you're talking about." There, that wasn't exactly a lie—April was a terrible liar—but it kept everything vague. She didn't want to lie and tell people the twins weren't Frank's, because she hoped to clarify the truth soon. They'd grow up knowing their father and knowing they had a place in the community and his family.

"Don't they ask about their dad?" Shelby pressed on.

April felt tongue-tied. The twins *were* starting to ask about their father, but so far, April had managed to put them off with vague statements like "he's a good man" and "one day you may get to meet him." In kindergarten last year, there had been loads of single parents, so many that it hadn't been an issue for the twins.

Here in a more rural area, there were probably more kids who had both a mom and a dad, and the twins would start to put their inquisitive minds to that puzzle. More reason to hurry up and reveal the truth to Frank.

But not by means of Shelby. April glanced around, hoping for an escape. The kids were happily cutting paper and gluing cotton puffs onto it, making snow. "I need to go talk with my cousin before things break up here."

"Oh, *Nadine*." Shelby sniffed. "That poor girl." She smiled expectantly at April, obviously waiting to be asked about the latest gossip.

Well, April wasn't going to bite. "It was nice to see you," she said. That much of a fib she could comfortably tell. She headed off to the circulation desk as Shelby went back to her mom friend. Within seconds, the two of them were gossiping, looking over at April in a way that made it clear they were talking about her.

As she approached the circulation desk, a voice behind her made the hairs on the back of her neck rise. Sure enough, it was Frank. He was carrying a stack of books toward the same desk she was approaching.

There was no avoiding him. He gave her a surprised smile and held up the books. "More research materials to read through this weekend," he said, indicating the books. "I have a couple more holds that came in."

"That should keep us out of trouble."

Then she blushed. What kind of trouble might they get into, after all?

The library hummed with business, patrons checking out books or talking quietly, with laughter and louder talk from the children's room. Nadine had a line of people waiting at the desk.

From the corner of her eye, she saw Shelby coming. She gave Frank a quick smile and wave. "Going to grab myself a couple of books before the kids are done," she said, and veered away from Shelby and him both.

Which might have been a mistake, because Shelby went right up to Frank and started talking.

April's heart sank. Surely the woman wouldn't ask Frank a direct question about the twins—would she?

She watched their conversation from behind a shelf, feeling like a spy—feeling like a fool and a bad person, too. She was living with the father of her children, only he didn't know it. It would only be a matter of time before he found out, and he ought to find out from her, not from small-town gossip.

She lifted her chin, straightened her shoulders and made one of those unwise promises to God. *If Shelby doesn't tell him, I'll tell him myself, and soon.*

She hadn't wanted to do that, hadn't wanted to get into the emotions of that conversation while they were working together on a deadline-driven project. But if she had to, she had to. The twins and their well-being came first, and that meant she needed to craft a careful explanation and present it to him in a way that didn't alienate him, at least not from the kids.

Shelby walked away and Frank continued standing in line, not looking particularly upset or surprised. So Shelby hadn't told him her suspicions. Phew.

But it was only a matter of time. April needed to plan a way to tell Frank the truth, and sooner rather than later. Maybe even this weekend.

* * *

On Sunday, Frank put into action his plan to keep a distance from April.

Working together was wearing on him. He kept noticing how pretty she was and admiring her intellect and talent. Admiring her mothering, too. It wasn't easy to be a single parent, he'd always figured that, but seeing her in action had cemented his view. It was a tough gig, not for the faint of heart.

He'd noticed April worrying about Eli and had heard a little bit about it. Found himself sympathizing with the little guy, who still didn't seem enthused about school.

But April's kids weren't his business. *April* wasn't his business, except in a professional capacity. So he took his own car to church, not offering her a ride, and then accepted his brother Alec's invitation to Sunday dinner.

That might have been a mistake. Zinnia, Alec's daughter, kept asking about Evelyn.

Why hadn't he brought her along? He had to explain that Evelyn had her own family and wasn't a part of theirs. And that left him wondering: Were April and her kids eating alone, when he could have easily asked them to join him at Alec's?

Watching his brother serve the food and offer a blessing, watching him hold his new baby while Kelly, his wife, ate her own food, all of it made him long for what he didn't have. Kids. A wife. A family of his own.

"I, um, invited someone over," Kelly said. She sounded uncharacteristically nervous. "She's really nice, and she's had a rough time of it."

Frank nodded absently. He was keeping an eye on Zinnia, who was playing with Dozer and trying to get him to connect with Kelly's therapy dog, Pokey.

"What she's trying to say, fool, is that she wants to set you up with Nadine," Alec said with a none-too-gentle clap on Frank's shoulder.

"Set me up? With who?"

The doorbell rang, and a woman Frank knew a little, from the library, came in. She'd brought a pie that looked homemade. Alec and Kelly greeted her and thanked her, and then asked Frank to show her to the kitchen and help her cut the pie.

Frank chatted with her, finding her perfectly nice outside of the library, just as she was inside it. She was friendly, but not gushy. He couldn't tell if she knew about the setup attempt, nor if she approved.

He didn't approve. She was a nice woman, but he didn't appreciate his sister-in-law pushing a potential partner on him without warning.

A little while later, as he was leaving, Kelly walked him to his car. "So, do you like her?" she asked. "I can set you two up on a date."

"I can set up my own dates," he said, feeling irritable.

"You *can*, but will you?" She put a hand on his arm. "I'm sorry if I'm interfering,

Frank. But I'd like to see you meet someone nice and settle down, like your brothers have. Everyone needs love in their life."

"I'll think about it," he said.

And he did think about it. He thought
about it a lot as he went home and, ignoring the sounds of laughter and shouting
from the twins outside, marched directly
to his office.

Then he tried to stop thinking about
it. He opened a file on his computer and
started making notes about the last section
of the book.

Dozer, out of harness, nudged at his leg.
When Frank didn't reach to pet him, he
flopped down, letting out a gusty sigh.

His sister-in-law was probably right: he
should start dating. It had been a year since
he'd been out on a date, and there was a
reason for that: his last few dates had been
disasters, partly because he'd been awkward about his balance issues and need
for a service dog. Women tended to either

back off or look at him with pity. Or else they just fell in love with Dozer, who was a charmer, and forgot about Frank entirely.

He got back into his work, focusing on the undercover sting that had resulted in the death of West Virginia's biggest fentanyl dealer. It had been a terrifying day. He knew he had courage and could rise to a challenge, and he'd done it. But courage didn't mean you weren't scared; it just meant that you took action anyway. He'd known the price might well be his death, and there were so many things he hadn't done that he wanted to do.

That was what had brought him back to Holiday Point more and more frequently during his recovery from an injury that had, initially, seemed like it could be fatal. Frank had deliberately avoided scrutinizing doctors' notes about his brain injury, because "brain bleed" and "likely permanent damage" weren't things you wanted to contemplate.

He'd forced himself to go over everything for this section of the book, the lead-in. But he hadn't yet written up his account of the actual day everything had come to a head. He knew that was what he needed to do next. It was the missing piece.

Every time he started work on it, though, he froze up.

Dozer trudged over to the window and jumped his front paws up to the sill. He stood there, woefully looking out, his expressive face occasionally turning back to Frank. Once, he barked.

Well, they couldn't have that, could they? Frank needed to take the dog out. A spin around the house, or maybe around the neighborhood, would settle his boy down.

Even as he put on a coat and hat and mittens, he knew he was fooling himself. He wasn't going out for Dozer's sake; he was going out for his own. He wanted to avoid working on the most painful section of his project. And he wanted to see the kids, and April.

As soon as they were outside, Frank

blinking in the bright, snowy landscape, Evelyn came running over. "Come on, Mr. Frank, you hafta go sledding with us!" Cute as a button in her puffy blue jacket, she held out a mittened hand.

He let her lead him toward April and Eli, who were at the top of a gentle slope that led to the neighbor's backyard. Dozer ran circles around them.

It was then that he realized the sleds were big pieces of cardboard. "I'm guessing we can borrow a real sled from next door," he said.

Both twins looked quickly at their mother.

"We're fine with our super-special, hand-crafted sledding devices, aren't we, kids?"

Evelyn nodded. Eli looked longingly toward the house next door.

"Your sleds are great," he acknowledged, and April's shoulders relaxed. She was touchy about her financial circumstances, he'd noticed. Determined to provide for her kids herself, not to take handouts.

Did the twins' father realize that they

were living at near-poverty level? Frank had grown up in a household that would be called "disadvantaged" today, and he recognized the signs: store-brand foods, bald tires on the vintage vehicle, an emphasis on cheap carbs like ramen and pancakes. April was trying hard, but wow, raising kids alone was expensive, and it didn't seem like she'd gone to college. His hat was off to her for finding time for a side hustle writing articles.

"Let's go!" Evelyn was jumping up and down, eyes sparkling. Nothing like an excited kid.

"I wonder if I can fit on those sleds, though," he said.

"We can get you a great big one! C'mon, Eli!" Evelyn ran to the stack of boxes that were waiting for the trash.

It was all the way out at the street. Frank started toward them, meaning to help.

April spoke up. "They'll be fine. Let's let them do it themselves."

He stopped, turned back and smiled.

"Very smart." She was. He'd met a few overly protective mothers and had read a few articles about helicopter parenting. That was a mistake, he felt, but you could go too far in the other direction, too: neglecting your kids' emotional and physical needs for weeks on end, as had happened with him and his brothers. Mom had tried, but she was also a functioning alcoholic with a pill problem on the side. Sometimes, the desire to escape had won.

Was it cause or effect that he and his brothers had been troublemakers? Maybe they'd been too much of a handful for Mom even as little kids. Or maybe her neglect, benign or otherwise, had led to them seeking attention elsewhere. They'd gotten plenty of it, mostly negative.

April seemed to be striking a nice balance. She watched the twins as they located and extracted a tall box from the recycling stack and pulled it over, and she expressed lavish admiration when they dropped it in front of the adults. Both kids were pink-cheeked and out of breath.

That was good parenting, too—having the kids get outside and do physical things. It was something a lot of busy parents didn't make time for these days. There was an epidemic of kids sitting inside for days at a time, pounding video games and ruining their health. That wasn't going to happen to this pair.

"Get on it, get on it," Evelyn half begged, half ordered.

What choice did he have? The worst that could happen was that he'd fall off in the soft snow and make a fool of himself.

Hoping his balance would hold, he climbed onto the cardboard box and edged it to the top of the hill. Eli coached from one side and Evelyn from the other.

"You hafta find a place to hold on," Eli said. He ran a practiced hand over the edge of Frank's box. "Like this. Here's like a handle."

Kid was right. He gripped the notch in

Eli's side of the box, and then Eli ran over to the other side. Together, he and Evelyn found him another likely handle while April watched from the side, smiling proudly.

She'd raised some great kids.

At the edge of the gentle slope, Evelyn patted his arm. "If you fall off, it's okay," she said. "What matters is you tried."

"If you're too scared, you don't hafta go," Eli said. "A little scared is okay 'cause then you get braver."

"Thank you," he said gravely to both of them. His mind swirled with admiration for April, because wisdom like that wasn't something six-year-olds would come up with themselves. Those were near-direct quotes of their mother, he was certain.

He pushed off and slid down, his weight taking him past the runs already packed down by the kids and April. He was almost at the edge of the river when he stopped himself by rolling to one side.

He shook his head a little. No dizziness. Amazing.

"Are you okay?" April stood above him, breathing hard. The kids followed close behind.

"I'm fine," he said.

"You almost went into the river!" Eli said, his forehead scrunched into a frown.

He smiled at the little boy. "I knew I could stop. I looked ahead and predicted that would happen. When it did, I was ready."

Eli frowned, looking thoughtful.

"Well, you worried us a little bit," April said. "I did a preliminary run and didn't even come close to the edge of the river, so I thought it was safe."

"Weight differential." Frank was probably heavier than the three of them put together. "You and the kids will be fine."

Only now did Dozer wander over and nose at Frank, still half on and half off of his sled. Frank rubbed the dog's head in thanks, then held on to his back to leverage himself up off the ground. "Beat you to the top of the hill!" he yelled, and took off, holding the cardboard, Dozer racing and barking beside him.

They all did a few more runs and Frank was pleased that there was no dizziness. April checked in with him about it, once. "Are you sure you're okay?" she asked.

"I am." He shrugged. "But that doesn't mean it's going away. I have good days and bad ones." He was saying it as much to himself as to her.

Finally, Eli flopped down in the snow. "I'm c-c-cold."

"Come have hot chocolate with us," Evelyn said, taking Frank's hand. "And Mom's making pizza. We're gonna watch a movie, too!" She sounded awed.

He looked over at April then, something he'd tried to avoid doing during this whole sledding escapade. Seeing her flushed and sparkly-eyed, her hair escaping out of its ponytail, laughing at her kids…each time he'd caught a glimpse, his mouth had gone dry.

He didn't need to be having those feelings for his co-writer. Nor for his ex-girl-friend who'd cheated on him once already.

Now she was watching him with her head tilted to one side, a smile playing on her lips. "You're welcome to join us," she said easily, surprising him.

Why was she saying that? Was she accepting him in as a family friend, good ole Uncle Frank, or was there something more to her invitation?

Wisdom dictated that he shouldn't find out. "If you have extra, I'd happily join you."

"Of course." She frowned a little. "We always have extra for our friends, right, kids?"

They both nodded without paying much attention. Clearly, this was another family value she was instilling in them. And having grown up as that extra kid who'd dined with a number of friends' families, he had to admire the generosity. He could still remember the few who'd turned him away after their kids had invited him to eat. He also remembered that, at his house, there hadn't ever been enough extra to share.

"I'm in, then. Thank you."

He helped the kids out of their snowsuits and went with them to select a movie from their stack of library DVDs. He could hear April working in the kitchen. The kids were warm, pressed against him, one on each side.

After they'd all drunk hot chocolate and while the homemade pizza was baking in the oven, the kids started the movie. Frank held back, rinsing mugs and loading them into the dishwasher. When he turned, finished, April was right behind him, inches away, and his instincts took over. He reached out and put a hand on her upper arm, looked at her lips and then into her eyes.

He started to lean toward her, but the expression in her eyes was stormy enough to stop him. They looked at each other for a long moment. Frank felt like she was trying to see into his soul, and he knew he was trying to see into hers.

What did any of this mean?

On the one hand, he wanted what he'd just had a taste of with April: to be a part of her little family, to play with and educate the kids, to share laughter together, to plan a fun night indoors.

On the other hand, did he let himself get closer when this was the woman who'd nearly broken him seven years ago?

He remembered like yesterday how he'd felt when he'd learned the truth of what she'd done. His heart had ripped, and the damage had been severe. Enough function was lost, enough of a scar remained, that he hadn't gotten that close to a woman again.

Now he felt like his heart was regenerating. But did he risk injuring it again?

He stepped back. "You know what, I'd better take a rain check on the pizza," he said. "I'll let the kids know." And he'd go call Nadine from the library, set something up. That would be much smarter and much safer than letting April weave her web around him again.

Chapter Seven

The next Saturday, April and the twins slept in. They'd just cleaned up after breakfast, midmorning, when car doors slammed outside.

Ugh. She'd hoped to have time to scour the local paper for places to live once this gig was over. She'd also planned to tell Frank that guests would be coming into their shared common space, but it was too late.

She'd put it off because she avoided talking with him about anything but work, and she'd tried to stay away from him in her off hours. And rightly so. He'd wanted to kiss her, she was sure of it. Even worse, she'd wanted to kiss him back.

That would be a mistake that could spiral into a disaster, not only for herself, but for her kids. Best to stay away, she'd thought. But she hated to bring guests into their shared dwelling without at least giving him a heads-up.

Wiping her hands with a dish towel, she beckoned to Evelyn. "Run and tell Mr. Frank we're having a meeting for a little while, in the kitchen. I think he's in his office upstairs." She actually *knew* he was in the office. She was hyperaware of his location in the house, and since she'd tried to stay away from him after-hours, she'd become even more attuned, much to her own dismay.

She walked to the door, Eli trailing behind her, and opened it just as the woman on the other side rang the bell. "Hi, Darci Mae, Emily. Come in."

The two women turned as one to the side yard, where their kids, both little boys from Eli's class, were running and sliding in the slushy, muddy snow. "Come on in, kids," Darci Mae said.

Did they really intend to bring their kids in here in that condition? "Let me get some towels so the boys can dry off," she said, and hurried upstairs to the bathroom.

By the time she got back, it was too late. Darci Mae's son—Bentley?—was running through the house, chased by a scolding Evelyn. The other boy stood patiently on the doormat.

"Go on and play," Darci Mae said to the boy waiting on the mat.

"Go ahead, Logan," the other mother said nervously.

"But let's wipe you off first." April hurried to him. "Thank you so much for standing on the rug. I really appreciate that you didn't get the house dirty." She handed him a towel. "Wipe off your feet and anywhere else that has mud on it, and then you kids can have doughnuts and milk in the kitchen."

"Okay," Logan said agreeably. His mother helped him wipe off, shooting anxious glances at the other woman.

Bentley's mom frowned. "I don't allow Bentley to eat processed foods," she said.

April restrained her eye roll. "That's fine. We have cheese sticks and grapes, too. Evelyn!" She reached for her daughter. "Please take Eli and Logan into the kitchen. You may get out our snack foods. Get out some grapes and cheese sticks as well as doughnuts. I'll be in to pour milk as soon as we get Bentley cleaned up."

"Oh, look at that," Darci Mae said as if she'd just noticed the streaks of mud that followed Bentley around. She didn't make a move to clean up, nor did she apologize.

If she were going to act as irresponsible as a first-grader, then April was going to have to treat her like one. She handed Bentley's mom the second towel she'd brought down. "If you could just wipe his feet, or even better, have him take off his shoes," she said, "I'll grab some paper towels to clean up the mud."

She found a roll of paper towels and started wiping streaks off the floor, reminding herself of why she'd had the mothers over in the first place. It would be nice for the twins to get to know some classmates better, and it would help all of them integrate into the community.

Darci Mae finished swabbing off her son and sent him running into the kitchen. She didn't follow him, and she didn't help April finish wiping down the entryway floor. Instead, she looked around the room, curiosity on her face.

Frank came in, wearing sweats, rubbing his chin. Dozer lumbered beside him without his vest.

Great. So Evelyn hadn't let Frank know guests were coming.

A surprised smile broke across Darci Mae's face. "Isn't this domestic and sweet?" she said in a tone that meant *Isn't this great gossip for me to share with the world?* "Hey, Lily," she called toward the kitchen. "Come meet April's...friend."

April shot Frank an apologetic look. "I'm sorry I didn't let you know I had company." April managed to keep her voice calm, but she knew her hot blush looked anything but calm.

Frank glanced quickly from April to Darci Mae and back again. "Not a problem. We'll work later," he said in an avuncular, boss-like voice. "Frank Wilkins," he said to Darci Mae, and reached out a hand for her to shake. After a moment, she did, and introduced herself.

He introduced himself to the other mom, Lily, which was good, because April couldn't have remembered the woman's last name if her life had depended on it. Then he grabbed Dozer's leash, shouldered into a jacket and took the dog outside.

April blew out a breath as she led Darci Mae into the kitchen, where the kids all sat at the table with doughnuts in front of them. The bowl of cheese sticks and grapes sat untouched.

"Can I get you ladies some coffee or

tea?" she offered. "And then we can sit in the living room and figure out our plan. Eli and Evelyn, if you want to show your friends your toys, you may take them to your room after you clean up."

A few minutes later, April flipped on the gas fireplace in the living room and then sat in a big, overstuffed chair. The other two mothers settled on the large couch.

Darci Mae was looking around the room with curiosity again. Clearly, she wasn't the type to get right down to business, but April had work to do. She jumped up, grabbed a note pad and sat back in her chair, tucking her feet under her. "We should get started while the kids are still acting civilized. Let's all share our ideas and we'll see where they come together." She outlined her own simple plan: an active game, a quiet craft and cookies.

Darci Mae's slight sneer said it all. "I'd like to see a valentines box competition. All the parents could vote with dollar bills, and we could donate the proceeds to a

local charity. We could celebrate which-
ever child raises the most money."

The thought of making two competi-
tion-worthy valentines boxes made April
cringe. "Lily, what about you? Ideas?"

"Hers sounds fine," she said, nodding toward Darci Mae. "Honestly, I've been too
overwhelmed to think of any party ideas."

"I love the idea of a charity involve-
ment," April said. "But making valentines
boxes could be a lot of work."

"Well, if you don't have time to plan the
party…" Darci Mae trailed off.

"No, I mean it's work for the parents to
make boxes. What if other classes ask for
fancy boxes and they have several kids?
What if they work a couple of jobs?"

Lily looked at April like she was a hero.
"What if they're just not artistic? I actu-
ally kind of like the quick and simple plan
April had."

Darci Mae shot her a look that said *I'll
deal with you later.* "I guess if people don't
have time to do something for their kids…"

"It's about priorities." April was obviously not endearing herself to Darci Mae, which had kind of been her goal. Oh, well. "Kids will be happy with a shoebox they decorated themselves and a packet of snack cakes from the grocery."

A sudden yell came from the kitchen—Eli—and all three of them jumped up and hurried in, April in the lead.

Darci Mae's son, Bentley, loomed over Eli, who sat in the corner, arms wrapped around his legs, shoulders hunched. Evelyn stood with her hands on her hips, yelling, "Stop it!"

Logan crouched by the back door, crying. "I wanna go home," he said when he saw his mom.

"What happened?" April rushed to the corner, nudged Bentley aside and pulled Eli to his feet. "Are you hurt?"

Eli shook his head, his eyes shiny with unshed tears.

"That boy called Eli a bad name," Evelyn reported, her voice indignant. "And he says we're poor."

A hand on Eli's shoulder, April looked at Darci Mae. "I wonder where he heard that?"

Darci Mae didn't look at her. "Did you say something unkind?" she asked her son.

"No!" Bentley crossed his arms over his chest.

Darci Mae turned to April. "He didn't do anything. Your son must be lying."

"One of them must be." And then April stifled the surge of defensiveness she felt on Eli's behalf. "I'll talk to Mrs. Constantine tomorrow and make sure she keeps an eye on the pair of them. She won't stand for bullying, I'm sure. Or tattling," she added, giving Evelyn a stern look.

"Eli was mean to *me*," Bentley fake-blubbered. He covered his face, then peeked out between his fingers.

April was the youngest mom there by a decade at least, but she once again took charge. "I think we've all had enough for today," she said. "We all expressed our ideas. Can we continue this with a video chat later in the week?" *That way, we won't have to get the kids together,* she thought. Her idea of helping the twins make friends quickly had obviously failed, although Logan had potential.

"But if we're having a valentines box competition, we need to get the word out," Darci Mae argued. "I for one am going to need a lot of supplies."

"We haven't decided what the party will be yet." With an effort, April kept her tone cordial. "Even if we decide to go with your idea, I think we should make it clear that the kids themselves should decorate the boxes."

When Darci Mae glared at her, she glared right back.

Eli was cowering behind her and Evelyn sulked at the table. The other two boys clung to their mothers.

"I'll text you both with some ideas for a meeting time," April said. At this point, she just wanted the other moms and kids out of the house. "We'll make it soon, in case we go with the box-decorating idea."

"Fine," said Darci Mae. She took her coat and her son's and left without even putting them on, let alone saying goodbye.

Lily offered April a tentative smile. "Thanks for having us," she said. "I'm sorry about…" She waved a hand toward the kitchen. "Come on, Logan," she said, and they went out to join the other family in their large SUV.

As April turned back to do damage control, she realized her plan had backfired. Rather than embedding herself and her kids more thoroughly into the community, she just might have made them seem like aliens.

Frank was editing one of the early chapters of the book, having taken April's suggestions, when there was a knock on the door. "I'm sorry that happened this morning," she said as she came in. "Hope you didn't get disturbed by the yelling."

He'd heard it, but it hadn't disturbed him. Not really. More disturbing was the way April looked in her sweater and faded jeans, her cheeks flushed, her hair mussed. Frank's throat went dry.

Which was *not* supposed to happen. After his near disaster of wanting so badly to kiss her that he'd almost done it, he'd stayed strictly professional for the past week.

This morning, since it was Saturday, he'd decided to loosen things up, maybe work by the fire, keep things light. But then her guests had come in. If Frank had to hazard a guess, it hadn't gone well.

His mind waged an internal war: Should he ask her to stay, enjoy her presence even if he couldn't do anything about it? Or should he try to get rid of her before he made a fool of himself?

"We don't have to work together today if the kids need you," he said.

"No, we should work. The kids are play-ing outside, and they know what to do when they get cold."

He raised an eyebrow. "First-graders can get out of their snowsuits by themselves?"

"They know to take off their boots, and they can change their clothes. I'll have to do some cleanup, but I was planning to mop the kitchen and living room today anyway. Our visitors brought in a little dirt."

"You don't have to mop! There's a clean-ing service."

She shrugged and waved a hand. "There's always plenty to clean when you have kids. I don't mind. Let's get started with your notes for the last quarter of the book."

Frank's stomach tightened. "That's a lot to get into today."

"We can start," she said.

Frank sighed and opened the file on his computer. It was supposed to contain about twenty thousand words; it had five thousand, and even those had been hard-wrung. He glanced out the window.

"Are you avoiding this part of the project?" she asked.

Frank was still looking out the window. "You know what," he said. "I think Eli would benefit from learning to deal with bullies from a man."

"You didn't answer my question."

"I guess that gives you your answer." He *was* avoiding the part of the book that dealt with the horrendous climax of the story they were telling. "I need to work on it. But not today."

"You're the boss," she said. "But to meet the deadline, we'll for sure need to complete that part next week."

"Deal." He stood. He couldn't wait to get out of that little room, get outside. "I could also work with Eli on his throwing arm," he said. "If he develops great skills in athletics, he'll be better able to fit in and avoid being bullied."

"More manly stuff?" she asked, raising an eyebrow as she stood.

He lifted his hands, palms out. "Hey, I'm sure you can do all this yourself. Just thought another perspective might be useful. I'll butt out."

"No." She put a hand on his arm but then pulled it back, her cheeks going pink. "I appreciate the offer, and I'd love to have you talk to Eli. But—" She held up a hand. "We girls want to play, too."

"I wouldn't have it any other way." And he meant it. He'd been involved in male-dominated units of the military and police, and he came from a family of four boys. But he definitely appreciated what women added to any activity or gathering.

As they walked out, he caught a whiff of flowers from her hair.

He swallowed hard. Yeah. He liked how good women smelled, too. April in particular.

Outside, the kids were sitting on the back stoop, apparently catching their breath after building something—he couldn't tell what—out of snow. "It's a snow dog!" Evelyn said indignantly when he asked.

He brushed snow off an Adirondack chair for April and then lowered himself into the other chair. "Want to know a foolproof strategy to deal with bullies?" he asked Eli.

"Yeah!" Eli said, closely echoed by Evelyn.

Frank had the feeling Evelyn would never have a problem with bullies.

"Let's do the talking strategy first," he said.

"What's a strategy?" Eli whispered to his mom, or tried to. His words were easily audible.

"It's a plan," April said. "Listen to Mr. Frank."

"When someone says something mean," he said, "the first thing to do is pretend you didn't hear them. Just say, 'What? I'm not sure I heard that right.'"

"But then they'll say the mean thing again," Evelyn said.

"Probably so. But it'll sound worse, and sillier, the second time. If other people are listening, they'll notice that."

"But…what do you do the next time they say it?" Eli looked concerned.

"Then you do the same thing again. Say 'What did you say?'"

Both twins seemed unconvinced. But Frank had learned this strategy from a female officer getting harassed in a mostly male unit, and he'd seen it work.

"Pretend I'm the mean guy," he said.

"I want to be the mean guy!" Evelyn cried. "Can I?"

"Sure," he said. "Say something mean."

April's eyes widened and she opened her mouth.

Evelyn said, "You're a crybaby!"

Eli burst into tears.

Whoa. Not a good start.

"I'm just pretending!" Evelyn put her

arms around her brother and stroked his hair.

"Sorry," Frank said to April, feeling contrite. "I have a lot to learn about kids."

"It's okay," April said, "but maybe one of the adults should say the pretend-mean thing."

"You do it!" Eli pointed at her, his tears forgotten.

"Okay." She frowned, her brow wrinkling. Then: "Eli, your hair is green!"

Eli's mouth dropped open and he looked at Evelyn for confirmation.

"Say the thing!" she told him. She put a hand to her ear to mime the correct answer.

Oh boy. He could imagine these two in the classroom, with their quick ways of communicating.

"I didn't hear you," Eli said to April. "What did you say?"

She played along. "Your hair is green."

Eli frowned, and for a moment, Frank worried that the little boy would take it to heart and start crying again. Maybe his strategy wasn't the best, but he'd told a couple of his nieces about it, and they'd said it worked. "What did you say?" Eli burst out.

"I said, your hair is green." April seemed to have a hard time keeping a straight face.

Evelyn burst out laughing. "Mommy is silly," she said.

Eli laughed, too. "She *is* silly!"

"She is." Frank smiled at her and then had to look away quickly. The sight of her pretty, laughing face did something to his heart.

Helping her kids did something to his heart, too. Man, he was soft. "You did good," he said to Eli. "Think you could do it at school?"

Eli shrugged. "Maybe I'll just hit that bully kid with a stick."

"Not a good idea," Frank said.

"No, Eli," April said at the same moment.

"But I want to be a soldier. Like him." Eli pointed at Frank.

"Soldiers don't hit people with sticks," Evelyn said. "They shoot them with guns."

"Did *you* do that?" Eli asked Frank.

Frank said, "Uhhhhh..." and looked at April. He needed help. Wasn't used to the blunt questions of kids.

"I'm sure Mr. Frank didn't use force unless it was absolutely necessary," she said crisply. She didn't look at him. He was obviously bungling this interaction that had been meant to help Eli.

"What's using force?" Eli asked.

Both twins looked expectantly from April to Frank and back again.

"It's like, hitting someone. You don't do it unless there's no other choice. You try to use words."

"Or the strat-gee," Evelyn said helpfully. "Say you didn't hear them."

"That's right," Frank said, relieved. "You should use the strategy and don't hit."

Eli looked unconvinced.

Sweat dripped down Frank's back. This kid-raising business wasn't for the weak.

He felt a new admiration for April, handling situations like this on a daily basis, figuring it out.

"We'd better go inside and get you dried off and warmed up," April said briskly, standing. The kids jumped up, too, and they headed inside.

Frank followed more slowly. April hadn't even looked at him. He got the feeling he hadn't impressed her today.

And unfortunately, he was starting to feel like impressing her mattered. A lot.

Chapter Eight

A week later, April was spooning oatmeal into three dishes when Frank walked into the shared kitchen. His hair was wet and he was rolling up the sleeves of his flannel shirt.

Deliberately, April slowed her breathing and looked away. No need to focus on how good he looked. During the week, she'd been able to keep her thoughts professional, but something about Frank's Saturday self was harder to resist.

"Mr. Frank! We're having oatmeal! Want some?" Evelyn was bouncing in her seat, but she didn't get up. She'd already gotten in trouble for running through the house and knocking over a lamp.

April smiled at her. "Good job staying in your seat, and offering food to Mr. Frank," she said. She hoped he would accept the offer of oatmeal, because she wasn't especially hungry for it herself. It was an economical breakfast, but they'd had oatmeal every day for a week. No matter how much she tried to dress it up with cinnamon or frozen blueberries, oatmeal was oatmeal.

"That sounds great," Frank said. He peered into the pan. "So that's how real oatmeal is cooked?"

"Real oatmeal? Ooohhh. Uh-huh. I'm guessing you're used to the instant kind."

"With fancy flavors like strawberries and cream."

"*We* have strawberries," Evelyn said proudly. "But today we're having banana-and-cinnamon flavor."

"Sounds good." He turned to April. "How can I help?"

"Put these on the table and slice this banana. You can split it between them."

"Got it." Frank did as he was told.

April pulled out an extra bowl and split the last of the oatmeal between hers and it, giving most of the cereal to Frank. Then she rinsed the pot in the sink.

Seeing Frank listen to the children's chatter as he helped with their breakfast made her feel impossibly conflicted. He was their father, but she was the only one who knew it. She was the only one who knew how natural it was for him to play this domestic role.

She carried the two remaining bowls to the table, poured Frank coffee and refilled the children's milk. After they held hands for a blessing, they dug in, and April found the oatmeal didn't taste quite so dull with Frank at the table.

She had to be losing it.

"So, there's a reason I came down," Frank said.

Dozer walked over and put his head on Frank's knee, looking up at him.

He laughed. "Right. I came down to feed you, but that's later. I actually wanted to invite you all to go hiking."

"Yeah!" Evelyn said.

"Yeah!" Eli echoed.

April gave him a scolding look, head tilted, eyebrows raised.

He read it instantly. "Oops. Sorry, kids. I need to talk this over with your mom first."

"You two have that play program at church," April reminded the twins.

"I don't wanna go," Eli said. "Wanna go hiking."

"Finish your breakfast. Mr. Frank and I will talk about it."

"We'll take our breakfast to the TV so you can talk," Evelyn offered, her expression speculative. They weren't normally allowed to watch TV in the morning. Nor were they allowed to eat a messy food like oatmeal in the living room.

"I'm done!" Eli scooped the last bit of oatmeal into his mouth.

"You may go watch TV for a few minutes," April said to him. "Evelyn, finish your breakfast."

Evelyn scarfed down her food, too. April debated correcting her manners but decided that wasn't a battle she wanted to fight today. A moment later, the twins' dishes were in the sink and they were contentedly watching TV in the adjoining room.

Before she could say anything to Frank, he held up a hand. "I'm sorry for springing this on you, and for telling the kids before asking you first. That was my mistake."

"Kinda." It was hard to stay mad at a man who apologized well.

And who looks so good doing it.

She hoped he didn't notice the heat rising in her face. "What about our work today? We got a lot done last week, but not enough. We need to get to that last section, and that was the plan for this morning."

She squinted at him. "Are you avoiding that material again?"

"Maybe a little," he admitted, looking sheepish. "We can work on it this afternoon, after the kids are worn-out. I guarantee that an outdoor excursion with my brother Cam's two boys will wear everyone out, even Evelyn."

"Hmm. Evelyn *is* pretty hyper this morning. And they'd both benefit from getting outside."

April wanted to get outside, too. She wanted to spend Saturday playing with her kids, not working.

The truth was, she wanted to spend time with Frank. Nonworking time. Fun time. She felt like she'd felt at eighteen, when this handsome, grown-up man had taken an interest in her, had invited her out.

She shouldn't cultivate that feeling; she should squelch it. A better person would insist that her kids stick to the church-related activity and would spend the day working as planned, even if her co-author decided to bail and go hiking. There was plenty she could do alone.

But there had been too little fun in her life since she'd become a single mom at nineteen. Too little fun for her kids, too, because she'd always had to work so hard and had lacked the funds for a lot of activities.

Here was something free and fun that she could do with her kids. The fact that Frank, who'd grown from that hot older man she'd fallen for years ago into an even hotter man who was also thoughtful and kind and heroic…

"You've been wanting to talk to Cam's wife, Jodi, about writing and blogging, right?" Frank said. "Well, here's your chance."

He was right about that. And the sun was shining, the sky blue. It was the kind of day that almost insisted you spend it outside. "We'll go, but you were still wrong to talk to them about it without checking with me first."

"I know. I was. How can I make it up to you?" His eyes darkened and there was a teasing look in them.

Her heart rate quickened and she took a step back. "You can make it up by promising to work hard all afternoon. We need to report our progress to your agent, and I don't want to make a bad report."

"It's a deal," he said.

Forty-five minutes later, they were at a local trailhead. Sunlight filtered down through pine branches, making diamonds in the snow. A chickadee landed on a low branch, calling *fee-bee, fee-bee* in its high clear voice.

Frank's brother Cam and his wife, Jodi, pulled in beside them, and their sons, Hector and JJ, spilled out of the back seat.

April hopped out of Frank's truck and turned to help the twins out, but they were already sliding down just as JJ had.

This was why it would be good for them to have cousins. Cousins they knew about, who could help them figure out life from a kid's point of view.

"Where's the baby?" Frank asked.

"Your mom's watching her," Jodi said. "Thankfully. It would be a pretty short hike with a four-year-old," she added to April.

"You let Mom watch her?" Frank frowned.

"At our house," Cam interjected. "No alcohol there. And Alec is gonna check in on her."

Interesting. April hadn't known Frank's mom had a drinking problem, but it didn't shock her. If anything would motivate her to stay sober, it would surely be her growing number of adorable grandkids.

April checked the twins' jackets and made sure their hats were tugged on snugly. "Wear your mittens, too," she commanded.

The twins glanced at the bigger boys, realized they were also wearing mittens, and put theirs on.

A coating of snow lay on every branch, creating a lacy pattern against the bright blue sky. The air felt cold and crisp, and the woods were silent except for the occasional birdsong and the excited shouts of the children.

The men led the way. Frank was larger-framed than Cam, but about the same height. They strode together, talking, the kids in front of them.

"Nice to see, isn't it?" Jodi asked. "I'm glad Frank is back. Cam missed him."

"Frank seems like he wants to settle down here," April said. "I think he should. Having his brothers nearby is a real blessing."

"And the kids love Uncle Frank," Jodi said. "I wish Frank would settle down and have some kids of his own. He's great with them." She watched as Frank knelt to adjust Eli's hat. "They look so cute together. Like father and son."

April's face heated and her stomach twisted. She studied Jodi's face, wondering if the comment meant she knew something. But she couldn't tell.

Frank *was* great with the kids, even just as a friendly adult in their lives. What right did she have to deprive him of them, and them of him? Looking at Jodi's open, kind face, she was tempted to spill the whole story.

But she had to tell Frank first. And as much as she wanted to do it soon, now, today, she knew she couldn't.

Frank was already dealing with a lot of emotional stress, revisiting difficult memories for the book. And the book's story really did need to be told. Moreover, they both needed the income from the book. They'd agreed not to discuss their past until the project was done.

As soon as they finished, she'd tell him.

For now, she needed to get Jodi on a different track of thinking, and she had just the way. "How is it, being a freelance writer and blogger in a town like Holiday Point?"

Jodi laughed. "It would be a disaster if I stuck to writing about and for Holiday

Point. But my blog's reaching a bigger and bigger audience. If you don't mind working remotely, then it's no problem to live and work here as a writer. Are you thinking about starting a freelance business here?"

And they were off, talking about it. April told Jodi about her parenting articles, and it turned out they'd written for a couple of the same publications. Jodi focused on books and reading, and was happy to hear that April had read and enjoyed her blog.

"It's great to talk to another writer," Jodi said. "We should meet up to write at the café sometimes."

"I'd love that. If it all works out for me to stay."

Jodi nodded speculatively. "So you'll be looking for a place to live once the gig with Frank is up?"

April nodded. "And for a job. Do you know of anything? The freelance stuff is extra, but I need that steady income and insurance coverage."

"I'm sure it's tough raising kids on your own," Jodi said. "I think they're looking for aides at the elementary school. That might be nice."

"I'd love that." April explained how she'd worked in child care while the kids were in it. "But then again," she said, "I've already gotten into a disagreement with another mom in the kids' class."

"Oh, no. Is it Darci Mae?"

"Yes!" April told Jodi about the disastrous meeting. "I'm hoping the rest of the work can be done virtually. We've exchanged some emails and we have a video meeting scheduled for early next week."

"Mom!" Hector ran over, holding a big rock. "Look what I found!"

Jodi turned to look, and April scanned ahead to make sure the twins were okay.

She didn't even see the big root that tripped her up in the middle of the trail. She windmilled her arms, trying to maintain her balance, but it was a losing battle. She pitched forward and landed on the hillside, sliding down, unable to stop herself in the mixture of snow and ice.

She heard one loud bark, and then a dark shape leaped over her. It was Dozer. He put on the brakes as soon as he'd landed on the ground in front of her, and she tumbled against his broad body. And stopped. The big dog had broken her fall.

Her head spinning, she sat up, one arm on the dog. She looked into his warm brown eyes. "You're the best boy. Did I hurt you?"

As an answer, Dozer licked her face.

She shifted her weight off the dog, making sure she could move her arms and legs. The others were soon beside her. "Mommy! Are you okay?"

"Mommy, Dozer saved you!"

"April, did you hurt yourself?"

"I'm fine," she assured everyone. But when Frank helped her up, she realized she wasn't fine. She'd twisted her ankle, and putting weight on it was painful. She held on to his arm and tried to hop up the hill.

"That's not going to work." He moved beside her, and a moment later, she found herself cradled in his arms, being carried up the hill.

How could he do it? She wasn't tiny. But he moved with ease, so April leaned her head against his broad chest and felt the steady beat of his heart. Just for a moment, she'd enjoy this feeling of being protected by someone stronger than herself.

She inhaled the smell of his aftershave and felt the working of his muscles. But as Dozer came up beside them, reality struck and she struggled free. "I'm sorry, you can put me down. What about your balance issues?"

He shrugged. "Not a problem," he said. His hands were on her shoulders. "Let's get you over to this rock, and I'll take a look at your ankle."

Jodi and Cam had gathered the children around them. "Your mom is going to be fine," she was saying.

Frank loosened her boot and felt her

ankle, his fingers gentle. "Does that hurt?" he asked as he probed. "Or that?"

He pressed gently on the side of her ankle, and pain shot through her. "Ow!"

"Okay. Sorry. Can you move the foot?"

She tried it and flinched. "I can, but it hurts a little. Not too bad. I don't think it's broken."

"Probably best to cut the hiking trip short and get you home, or to the hospital."

"Home," she said quickly. She hated to admit that she didn't have insurance coverage. The kids did, due to a free program, but she'd had to rely on her own good health and God's protection.

Her kids, along with Hector and JJ, were standing with Jodi, watching from the other side of the trail. She smiled and held out her arms, and they ran to her. "Are you okay, Mommy?" Eli asked.

"I'm going to be fine. I just sprained my ankle."

Both kids looked worried. At that age, they tended to think parents were invincible, and seeing their mother hurt was scary.

Her desire to ease their fear made her forget the throbbing in her ankle. "You might have to bring me things while I rest on the couch." She tweaked Eli's nose. "You up for waiting on me, buddy?"

He smiled and nodded. "I'll help."

"Me, too, me, too!" Evelyn pushed in front of Eli.

"Of course you will. You're good helpers." She hugged them tight, then released them and studied their faces.

Her lighthearted approach had worked. Both children looked relieved.

"Where's Dozer?" she asked. "He's the real hero. I hope I didn't hurt him when I fell into him."

Frank whistled, and Dozer trotted over to them. "He's fine," Frank said. "He's a tough boy."

"He's a good boy." April rubbed the dog's big, blocky head, and the dog panted, seeming to smile. She looked up at Frank.

"He's amazing. It really seemed like he saw that I was falling and ran to help."

"He did." Frank knelt and rubbed the dog's sides. "That's what he's trained for, and he's caught me a few times. And rottweilers are protective. He must think of you as one of his responsibilities now."

"Well, I'm buying him a new box of dog bones next time I go to the store."

Jodi came over. "Evelyn and Eli, could you go make sure Hector and JJ are ready to go back?" She pointed down the trail, where the boys had gone to explore an uprooted tree. Once the kids had run off, she studied April with concern. "I'd like to take the twins home with us for the rest of the day," she said. "That way, you can get some rest and maybe visit the doctor."

"That's such a sweet offer, but you don't need to do that. I can manage."

"Of course you can manage," Jodi said, "but knowing the kids are cared for and having fun might be a help."

April didn't want to impose, but when she moved her ankle again, experimentally, pain shot up her leg. "Well...it would be, that's for sure. Thank you."

"And it'll give Frank the chance to take care of you." She winked, then turned toward the kids. "Hey, Evelyn and Eli. Would you like to come play with the boys this afternoon? We're stopping for burgers on the way home."

"Yeah!" Evelyn jumped a little, obviously happy.

"Mom might need us." Eli gave a worried look toward April.

"It's okay, honey," April said. She knew it was best for the kids, and it *would* be a relief, but on the other hand...it would also give her and Frank some time alone. Which could be good or bad.

It'll be good for working on the book, and that's what matters.

But the mixture of nerves and excitement that unsettled her stomach wasn't about the book.

* * *

This was bad.

Frank was helping April hop from the car to the house, and her tight grip on his arm felt way too pleasant.

He enjoyed being of use. That had always been important to him. It was one of the reasons he'd gone into the military and then law enforcement, and he was just realizing how diminished he'd been feeling, not being able to help anyone else. Being the recipient of assistance rather than the provider didn't sit well with him.

So maybe that was why helping April up the steps and into the house felt so great.

Don't kid yourself. You like being close to her, period.

After sweating on the hike and then cooling down in the car, walking through the wind felt harsh despite the sunshine. A loon called out from the direction of the icy river. Otherwise, town was quiet.

"Thanks," April said at the door. "I appreciate your getting me home."

If she was dismissing him already, he wasn't having it. "Let's get you settled down on the couch," he said, and guided her across the kitchen and into the living room. He helped her out of her coat, and when she pulled off her hat, he couldn't help but breathe in the flowery fragrance of her hair. He eased her down onto the couch, holding both her hands, then got a footstool for her ankle.

He flicked on the gas fireplace. "I want to take a look at that ankle," he said, "but can I get you some tea or a soda first?"

"You don't have to wait on me," she protested, then smiled and added, "but if you insist, a glass of cold water would be great."

In the kitchen, he got them both glasses of water, taking deep breaths, trying not to think about how it had felt to carry her to safety. Trying not to think about the fun of having breakfast with her and the twins in this very kitchen.

He handed her their waters and then

knelt beside the footstool. He unwound the hastily done wrap and studied the ankle. "Not much bruising, but it looks pretty swollen. Are you sure you don't want to go to the Quick Clinic?"

"I'm sure."

That answer had come too fast. "Are you afraid of doctors?"

"No!" she said vehemently. Then she added in a much lower voice, "I don't have insurance."

"Oh, wow." He hadn't even considered that, but of course. "You gave up your full-time job to come here," he said. "Along with its benefits."

"Right. But I'm fine. It's not that bad."

"I can pay. I *should* pay, since my project is the reason you don't have benefits. Not to mention the reason you were hiking in the woods in January."

"Frank. It's fine."

He poked at the ankle a little, noticing when she winced. She was right: it didn't seem to be a severe strain. "I'll wrap it up better and get you some ice," he said, and did so, ignoring her weak protests that she was fine.

He *tried* to ignore how good it felt to take care of her. She'd cheated on him before, he reminded himself. No matter how sweet she seemed, she was capable of betraying those she cared for. He'd be a fool to put himself in line for that trap again.

When he'd finished, she adjusted the ice pack on her leg and then looked at him. If he was hoping for a little return spark from her, he didn't see it. "Ready to get to work?" she asked.

"What?"

"The book. We need to move forward on it."

"But you're hurt." He'd welcome the chance to stay and keep her company, but digging into the end of the book didn't sound very appealing.

"My foot is hurt, not my brain or my writing hand," she said, and gave him a level stare. "I think you're still stalling. I think you're just scared."

"I'm not…" He looked into her eyes and couldn't lie to her. "You're right. I just…" He shook his head. "I have to admit, I hate the thought of reliving those experiences again. And organizing them into something coherent just means smacking myself over the head with it over and over again."

Her eyes were sympathetic. "Why don't you just tell me what happened? I can take notes. Record what you say in case I miss anything. I'll type it up and put it in order, and then you can read through it and tell me what I got wrong."

Her idea made sense. It was more than generous, since it put a lot of the work squarely on her shoulders. But the idea of blurting out everything that had happened turned his stomach. "I don't know if I can do it." He reached down automatically, and when his hand encountered Dozer's head, he felt a little better. The rottweiler was supposed to be a brace-and-mobility dog, and he was, but he provided a lot of emotional support as well.

And then suddenly, April's hand rested on top of his. "Frank," she said, "you have to talk about what happened if you're to get the book out there. And from everything I've read so far, it's a story that needs to be told."

He looked up, and there were those pretty blue-green eyes, calm and compassionate.

"I'll be right there helping you," she said. "And I won't judge."

Something about how she said it loosened the knot in his stomach. "Okay," he said. "I'll try."

He helped her hop to the desk and then sat down on the couch beside it. Dozer pushed his way in between the couch and the coffee table, and Frank rubbed the big dog's head. "I feel like I should lie down," he joked, looking at April. "So you could psychoanalyze me."

She laughed, a musical sound that made him smile to hear it. "No skill in that area," she said, "but I'm a good listener. Just start with the day it happened, and tell me everything you remember. I don't have to record it if you don't want me to."

He waved a hand. "Record away but promise me no one but you will see the transcript," he said. "This might be pretty choppy."

Dozer plodded off to his favorite spot on the rug and flopped down onto his side.

Frank drew in a breath and started. "We'd been working on this case since the beginning of my time in West Virginia. It was my first big case." He paused. "And my last."

She looked up at him quickly. "I'm sorry it was your last," she said. "That must be hard for you."

He nodded. "I expected to be a cop for the rest of my working years." The thought that he wouldn't gave him a hollow feeling, even now, as if the core of who he was had been extracted from him.

Some cops were killed in the line of duty. He should be grateful that he hadn't been, and grateful for the disability payments he received. He should dive into another career now, become a teacher, say, or do something with the courts, like victim advocacy.

But he'd always seen himself as a protector, from his childhood trying to deflect his father's anger away from his mother and brothers, to his days as an offensive tackle protecting the quarterback. He'd thought to carry on that role by working in law enforcement.

That wasn't an option now, so who was he? What was he supposed to do with his oversized, physically flawed self?

A lot of ex-cops went into security, but with his balance issues, there was no way.

"Hey." April tapped his upper arm. "You're thinking too much. Just tell me what happened."

So he did.

It had been a beautiful spring day, and Frank had felt good. Adrenaline high, of course, like it always was in undercover work, but he'd hoped this would be the big day. He'd been making buys from a particular seller, Big Hoss, for weeks, in gradually increasing quantities. Finally, the seller's supplier had wanted to meet him.

They'd had a sting planned, with good backup. Frank had approached Big Hoss's front porch and gotten his first surprise: the man had been out there, with a heavily pregnant woman whom he'd been helping into a chair.

Frank's stomach had knotted up then, and it knotted up now.

"So the guy, the seller, was acting all sweet and gentle and new-dad-like?" She was typing rapidly, the keyboard clacking.

"He was. Which seemed weird. But Big Hoss was all friendly, introducing me, inviting me in. Said the supplier was inside."

"Wow." She looked up from the computer screen. "What did you do?"

"Because she was there, I had to think on my feet." He was starting to sweat, just thinking about it. He reached down and put a hand on Dozer's head.

"How did you dress, when you were undercover?" April asked suddenly.

"Like a backwoods hick with a bad attitude," he said, his voice wry. "And I'm quoting my old partner. He got a kick out of it. Flannel shirt and jeans, beard down to here." He held a hand at collarbone level to illustrate.

"Wish I'd seen that version of you," she said, grinning. "You'd make a good mountain man."

"You wouldn't have wanted to see that." He shook his head. "I terrified children."

She laughed, then made a circling gesture with her hand, the universal signal to get on with it. "What happened next?"

He sucked in a breath. He'd gone this far; he could finish the story, at least the basics. "I was coming up the steps when the pregnant lady said she wanted to go inside. I thought Big Hoss would want to keep her out of it, but he helped her up and she went on ahead."

"So…how'd you deal with the change of plans?"

He nodded and closed his eyes, remembering. "I was wearing a wire, so I gave the code for the team to hold off."

She raised her eyebrows.

"Coughing fit," he explained.

"Did you consider backing out?"

He shook his head. "I pretty much had to go through with it at that point. If I'd backed down, he'd probably have shot me."

"Sounds scary."

"You go on autopilot. I was good at that, because of my time in a war zone. I followed him inside, and there's the pregnant lady pulling out the supplies, chatting with a supplier I recognized from our most-wanted list. Which made it bigger than I'd even guessed." He frowned. "That would have been great, but I was worried about the pregnant lady."

"Sounds like she was in on it all."

"Up to the neck," he said. "In fact, she's the one who pointed a gun at me. Said, 'I never did like your looks, but I especially don't like them today. Seeing your cash might change my mind about it.'"

He told it to April then, the bare bones of the story. How he'd had a choice to make, fast and with an audience. He'd been pretty sure he could disarm her, but Big Hoss and his supplier had been another story—both armed, obviously, and both ruthless.

And then a young, sleepy teenager—he'd later found out the kid's name was Elijah Lee—had walked into the room, rubbing his eyes, and it had all gone haywire when he'd said, "Mom?"

"I told you to stay in the bedroom," she'd screamed.

Thankfully, the team had heeded his warning to stay back. As it turned out, that delay had probably saved their lives.

Big Hoss had raised his gun, pointing it at Elijah Lee, but watching Frank. The pregnant mother of Elijah Lee had dived in front of her son. Trained to protect, Frank had gone for the dealer and they'd exchanged fire.

Once he'd gone that far, Frank dropped his head into his hands, remembering it all too vividly.

"You're doing well," April said quietly. "Tell me what you were thinking and feeling, if you can."

"I figured I was dead," he told her. "The supplier wouldn't be there without some protection of his own, but I just tried to cover the woman until she could crawl away. Only I got shot."

"What about your team?"

"They were able to take the supplier's guys into custody without anyone getting injured." He looked up at her, then back down at the floor. "And that's about all I remember."

When it was all over, the dealer was dead, Frank was unconscious and the pregnant mother lay bleeding with Elijah Lee hunched over her. Frank's colleagues had arrived and taken the supplier into custody. At least, that was what he'd pieced together after the fact.

Frank had woken up in the hospital with a brain injury caused by a gunshot that should have killed him. He'd asked after Elijah Lee and insisted on being taken to visit the children's floor, where the boy had been held for observation; he'd sustained a minor scalp injury after being grazed by a stray bullet.

It had been a groggy visit for both of them, but at least he'd seen for himself that Elijah Lee was going to be okay. Later, he'd learned he'd been taken in by his grandmother, and he'd gotten her address.

Elijah Lee's mom had been taken to a

different hospital. She hadn't survived and neither had the baby. Killed by a ricocheting bullet. And though the investigation had shown, definitively, that the kill shot hadn't been his, he still blamed himself.

He should have been able to save the woman and especially her unborn child, who now wouldn't have the chance to make something better of himself.

It had been a boy; he'd asked.

For a while after that, he'd been consumed by rehab from the vestibular issues caused by the brain injury, and then the process to get disability payments and a service dog. It had taken a few months, but when he'd gotten on his feet financially, he'd started sending money to Elijah Lee's grandma. He believed in helping others, and for him, doing it in a personal way, close to home, beat sending a check to a big impersonal organization. She'd written him the occasional letter back, expressing thanks and letting him know a little bit about their lives now.

They were doing okay. But he hated the thought that if he hadn't walked up to that porch, Elijah Lee would have still had a mom. For however long her lifestyle permitted, at least.

"All of it made me think," he said to April, after he'd told her the whole story. "I had to reassess what I was going to do with my life."

"What did you figure out?" she asked. She had that cute, serious frown, like she really wanted to know.

"Still working on it."

"With the book?"

"That's therapy," he said. "Coming back to Holiday Point, spending time with my family, that's where I'm at right now."

And it was leading him to the notion that he wanted to settle down and have a family, too. A brush with death left you hyperaware of what was important. For him, it wasn't going to be building a big police career, but maybe he'd like to build a family.

"I think your story is amazing," she said quietly. "It was hard, and you've certainly paid a heavy cost, but your work led the way to getting a big cartel out of the region."

"Right. I guess. I don't like killing—hate it, in fact—but I'm glad that dealer and his supplier aren't out there preying on more people." He moved up to sit beside her. "Thanks for listening. Every other time I've tried to talk about it, I've gotten this weird sharp pain in my head. That didn't happen this time."

"I'm glad. And I admire what you did. You sacrificed yourself, your health, to save that kid."

He'd always focused on the ones he'd lost: the pregnant woman and her baby. True, she'd made her own choices and she'd seemed okay with dealing dangerous drugs. But women in that world were vulnerable. Who knew what had happened to put her in that position?

No one would ever know now.

"Do you stay in touch with that kid?" she asked. "What was his name, Elijah Lee?"

He shook his head. "I followed what happened to him, through his grandma, but I haven't made contact since seeing him in the hospital two years ago." How had that much time gone by?

She looked thoughtful. "If you wanted to, it might be good for you. And not to be all commercial about it, but it could be good for the book as well. An epilogue, say. If you'd both be comfortable with that. We don't have to use his name. Probably shouldn't."

"You think I should visit him?" As he contemplated it, certainty came to him: it was the right thing to do. Felt it, like the heavenly father was pointing down, saying, *This. Do this.*

"I don't know how it would work out," he said, "but it would be good to try. Thank you for the idea."

Her smile was brilliant. "I'm even more excited to finish the book now." She made her way over to the couch and hugged him. "Thank you for telling me your story. I'll try my hardest to do it justice."

He had no intention of clinging on, but his arms had a will of their own. And once she was in his arms—with no objection; he made sure she was hugging him back—he automatically wanted to kiss her.

He smoothed back her hair, and she looked up at him.

There was friendship and compassion in her eyes, but there was heat, too. She was drawn to him. She wasn't pulling away.

He knew there were reasons he shouldn't proceed in the direction he wanted to go, but he couldn't quite remember what they were. Couldn't think, really, not while he was inhaling the fragrance of her hair and feeling the warmth of her, so comforting in the chilly room.

Frank was a man of action, always had been. He looked into her eyes for another moment, making sure she was okay.

Her beautiful mouth curved into a slight smile.

He lowered his head and kissed her.

Chapter Nine

Kissing Frank was nothing like she remembered.

It was much, much more intense.

As his strong arms wrapped around her, she felt something deep inside her relax. *This* was where she was supposed to be.

She touched the rough stubble of his cheek, the thickness of his neck and shoulders. Frank was strong, so strong. He'd actually picked her up and carried her up the hill after she'd fallen, and it had seemed like nothing to him.

She inhaled the scent of him and it cast her back to earlier times. A nervous feeling rose in her: What would he expect, here in the house alone, kissing her? After all, he was the father of her children.

But she couldn't make herself push him away, and slowly, she relaxed. His lips were firm, searching, but he didn't press for more. He wasn't making assumptions based on their past mistakes.

He was a good man.

With tenderness, he brushed back her hair. "I've been dreaming of this," he murmured. "You're so beautiful, April. I love holding you."

That, too, she remembered: that he was full of praise and encouragement, that he was surprisingly expressive in moments like these.

No wonder she'd never wanted to kiss anyone else.

She felt like she was at the top of the world's biggest roller coaster, about to experience the wonderful, terrifying downhill ride. This was dangerous, way too dangerous for a woman who had ultimate responsibility for two young lives. There were reasons—she could almost remember them—why she should stop this kiss right now.

But as his lips moved over hers, her intellectual decision to keep things professional flew away. He murmured sweet words, and she gave herself fully to the emotions rising in her.

This was the father of her children. This was the only man she'd ever kissed.

This was where she belonged.

Finally, he lifted his head and smiled at her. "You're an incredible woman," he said. "I feel so blessed to be here with you, right now."

She felt her own lips curve into a smile. "I feel blessed, too."

He shifted to pull her into a more comfortable position, curved into him, her back braced by his arm. Their faces were inches apart. "If I'd remembered just how good it felt to kiss you, I could never have held back as long as I did." His thumb brushed

over her lips, gently. "It's even better now."
He dropped a light kiss on her lips, and it
could have gone on if she'd encouraged
him.

But she pulled back and tilted her head
to lean against his chest. Right now, she
wanted to feel his strength. "I loved everything about being with you when we
were together before, and it does feel better
now." Because they were adults. Well, he'd
been an adult back then, but she'd been
little more than a high school kid, defy-
ing her father. Now, there was none of that
baggage.

Of course, there was other baggage, a
lot of it. The twins. The thought of them
sobered her, grounded her.

She wanted to settle down in Holiday
Point. She wanted the unconditional love
she'd never had. Maybe, just maybe, she
could have that with Frank.

But only if she could find out why he'd
left before.

She kissed his lips, just lightly, then

pulled away as his hands started to tighten around her. There wasn't going to be a round two, not until she knew more.

"It was good before," she said. "It was wonderful, but then you were gone. You left. How come?" They'd agreed not to discuss the past, but that had been before they'd kissed.

His expression cooled a little. "You have to ask?"

Her chest tightened and she pushed back her hair, suddenly too warm. "Yes, I have to ask. I have no idea why you ghosted me when things were so good between us." Because they *had* been good. After the night when they'd gotten carried away, they'd spent even more time together. Not in a room alone, though. They'd both known, after the one time together, what kind of heat would ignite if they went there, and how quickly.

So they'd taken long walks and shot baskets and eaten ice cream cones, gone to music-in-the-park nights, talked over late-night coffee at the diner. They'd gotten to know each other better, sharing their hopes and dreams and questions.

And then she'd found out she was pregnant. She'd hidden in her room for a couple of days, terrified her father would somehow be able to look at her and know. She'd ignored Frank's calls and had talked and prayed with a church friend.

It hadn't taken long for her to realize that she missed Frank and that she was wasting the last couple of weeks they had together. His leave would end, and he'd have to go back to his base.

She'd known she needed to tell him she was pregnant, and they'd needed to talk about the future. But when she'd gone to his parents' house, she'd learned he had left town. No forwarding address. His leave hadn't been over yet, but no one would tell her where he was spending the end of it. He hadn't wanted her to know.

The misery of that abandonment echoed in her, and she studied him. "You never answered my question. Why'd you disappear?"

He shifted away, stared off toward the window for a moment and then looked back at her. "Why'd you cheat, if it was so good?"

The words hit her like sharp, jagged rocks being thrown, one after the other. He thought she'd cheated?

How could he possibly think that? What had she ever done that would have led him to believe something so false?

Hope rushed out of her, like air from a rapidly deflating balloon. "How could you say that?"

He opened his mouth like he was going to speak, then closed it again and looked away, his mouth twisting, shaking his head.

Dozer came over and stood beside Frank, whining a little.

She felt like a child whose mother had been taken away from her. The ache was that deep.

She was supposed to be strong and independent. She ought to stand up and walk away.

But her legs felt too weak, her heart too empty. That brief moment of having him again, thinking it could possibly work between them, had made his harsh words all the more bruising.

Her phone buzzed, distracting her from the pain. Reflexively, she apologized. "I'm sorry, I have to get that, it might be about the twins."

The twins who are your kids, you jerk.

"Get it. That's fine." He scrubbed a hand over his face—trying to rid himself of all trace of her, no doubt.

The name that flashed on her phone took a minute to register. "LaWanda Gilbert… Wait, that's your agent. Why's she calling me?" She clicked into the call. "Hello?"

"April! LaWanda here, checking in on our project. I thought I'd better get your perspective. How's that big old bear treating you?"

Well, he just kissed me and dissed me, so... "Things are going okay," she said.

"Just okay?" LaWanda's voice sharpened. "What's wrong?"

April sucked in a breath and let it out slowly, trying to think. "Um, well, we just had kind of a breakthrough with the ending. But it's going to take a lot of work to get it done."

Frank was leaning forward, elbows on knees, cheeks on upraised hands. He didn't look at her, but his expression told her he was listening.

And she needed to pull herself together. This was business. This was food in her children's mouths. This was an opportunity to make a fresh start for them. "We'll get it done," she said, her voice firm. "Now that we've pushed past a pretty big sticking point, the rest is just details."

He raised his eyebrows, obviously doubting her claim, and April hated that she was so attuned to him.

"Is he there? Let me talk to him."

April handed the phone to Frank, and he took it just as the doorbell rang.

She started to push herself to her feet, winced and sank back. She'd barely remembered her sprained ankle.

He held up a big hand like a stop sign. "I'll get it." He walked to the door, talking to LaWanda. Dozer wasn't in harness, but he still walked beside Frank, and when Frank lurched a little, Dozer was there to steady him.

April leaned against the back of the couch, her thoughts in turmoil.

Why, oh, why had she let things go this far? And why did he think she'd cheated? Did he have that little knowledge of who she was?

If he only realized that he'd been her first and only. That she hadn't even gone on a date since her experience with him. Too grief-stricken at losing him, too terrified of how to make it, pregnant, in a big city. Too busy raising twins and supporting them on her own. The thought of meeting men and dating had barely crossed her mind, and when it had, she'd thought of Frank and shoved the whole notion aside as fast as possible.

Frank opened the door, and his brother Fisk came in, a first aid bag in hand. Frank gestured toward her.

Fisk came over. "So you had a fall?"

"I did." She swallowed hard. Time to playact like there was nothing wrong, because that was going to be a big part of her job for the next little while. She looked inquiringly at Fisk's medical bag.

"I was a medic in the army," he explained. "Loved it, and now, in my spare time, I'm training to be a volunteer paramedic."

"That's great." She was pretty sure that Fisk, who ran his own carpentry business and was raising a child, didn't have a whole lot of free time.

Plus, Fisk had a marriage to tend to. Unlike Frank, he'd found a woman he trusted and married her. He hadn't made baseless accusations, of that she was sure.

Fisk unwrapped her ankle and studied it, poking it here and there, gauging her reactions. Finally, he nodded. "There's some bruising, but not a lot. I don't think it's a major sprain, and it's definitely not broken."

"So... I can just kind of go on with life?"

"No. Not at all." He was rewrapping the ankle as he spoke. "I'll get you more ice, and you need to keep it wrapped and elevated. If you stay off it for a few days, it should heal quickly."

"I have six-year-old twins," she said. "Mothers of six-year-olds don't stay off their feet."

Frank was off the phone and walking slowly over to join them, Dozer close to his side.

"Bro, you're going to have to wait on her," Fisk told him. "She shouldn't be walking at all, but if she needs to, I'll dig up a pair of crutches she can use."

"Sure." Frank's voice was expressionless.

Dozer leaned against the couch in front of April and looked up at her as if to offer his assistance as well. She rubbed his soft ears. "You're such a good boy," she whispered to him.

"For now," Fisk lectured on, looking at Frank, "get her some ice and stop trying to make her work. She needs to rest, watch TV, take a nap."

"You're right," Frank said. "I should have known better." He headed into the kitchen, his words echoing behind him, bearing all kinds of meaning beneath the surface.

"I mean it, April. Take it easy and rest if you don't want this to drag on. I'll be back to check on you tomorrow."

"You don't have to—" she started to protest.

He raised a hand, stopping her. "I'll be back tomorrow. It's what we do in this family."

She looked at him quickly, to find his thoughtful eyes watching her. Did he know about the twins, know she was a legitimate part of the family through them?

She faked a smile and then, as Fisk left, waving off her attempt to stand, she pressed her lips together.

Frank had gone on the defensive about her cheating when she'd asked him why he'd left. He was just trying to shift the blame onto her. She'd seen her father do the same a million times.

There was no point in confronting a man who had those kinds of tendencies. When he came back in with an ice pack, she took it from him and put it on her ankle. Then she shifted her expression to neutral and looked at Frank. "Let's forget this happened," she said, waving at the seat beside her.

His eyes darkened. He obviously knew exactly what she was talking about: their mistake of a kiss.

She scratched her fingers down Dozer's broad back, and the rottweiler panted up at her with what looked like a smile. It gave

her courage. "If we keep things impersonal, we can finish the book on time," she
said. "That's important. I'll work through
my notes in the next couple of days, which
I can do without your input, and then I'll
bring them to you and you can edit. Just
like we planned."

"Just like... Sure. That sounds good."
His voice and face were still expressionless, mostly, but she could read him. He
was angry, and something else. Hurt?

Well, fine. If he was hurt, it was nothing
compared to how she'd felt, pregnant and
alone, when he'd dumped her. She leaned
over, grabbed her laptop and pretended to
type until he left the room.

Even at church the next day, even knowing that as a Christian he was supposed to
forgive, Frank still stewed.

What did *she* have to be mad about?

He'd been careful about kissing her.
Well, sort of. He'd checked in, twice, to
make sure she was on board. When you

were a big hulk of a guy like him, you could be intimidating, and he had never wanted even a hint of that.

She'd seemed fine with it. She'd enjoyed kissing him, hadn't she? He thought of the soft look in her eyes, the hitch in her breathing, the way her arms had wrapped around him, hugging him back. Yes, she'd been into it.

So if it wasn't that she was mad he'd kissed her, then what?

He shouldn't have come out with that direct of an accusation, he supposed. She'd gotten immediately angry, which had of course been a defense mechanism. Since then, she'd gone cold.

Well, fine. If she wanted to push off blame for their past relationship failure on him, she could go for it.

It was a good reminder that he shouldn't get involved with her again. This time, a relationship-plus-breakup would be worse, because there were a couple of kids who could get hurt.

As if magnetically drawn by the thought, Eli came over to where he and Dozer occupied a back row. The kid climbed up on the pew beside him and started playing with a small army jeep.

Frank looked around and realized that services had ended while he was stewing. He shot up a quick apology to God. He should have been paying attention, learning, praising. Not ruminating over some mistake he'd almost repeated.

He wanted to move on, have a family like his brothers. He'd had the thought, for just a moment, that he could do it with April.

But he couldn't, no matter how sweet her kids were. He ruffled Eli's hair. "How's it going, kiddo?" he asked, conscious that this bit of a relationship he'd developed with the twins would soon be ending.

Eli shrugged and glanced around, then slid to the floor and started driving the jeep along Dozer's back.

"There you are!" The scolding voice

belonged to a woman named Zoey, who taught one of the Sunday school classes. "Eli, you can't hit, and you can't hide."

Frank blinked. "You hit someone?" he asked Eli.

Eli nodded, still aimlessly running the jeep back and forth on the edge of the pew. "Why?"

Eli didn't answer at first, but then he held up the jeep. "He had this, and I wanted it. He wouldn't give it to me when I asked nice."

"Look," Zoey said to Frank, "I need to clean up the classroom. Can you let April know what happened?"

"Don't tell Mommy!" Eli hid his face with his hands.

"Tell her to call me." Someone beckoned to her from the side door of the sanctuary. "I need to go."

"Sure, I'll tell her," he said, and she hurried away.

Great. Everyone in Holiday Point seemed to think he and April were an item.

He saw April up front, talking to Nadine and Fisk. She was sporting a pair of crutches. Against his own wishes, he felt sorry for her, wanted to help her.

But she wouldn't welcome that, and it was only drawing out the pain. "Hey, Eli. If you tell your mom what happened, she might not be as mad."

Eli peeked up between his fingers. "She will be."

"She's going to find out anyway. If you tell her, and say you're sorry, that's the best thing." He saw Evelyn through the side door. "Better go now, before Evelyn gets to her and tells her."

He stood to leave, and Dozer lumbered to his feet and followed. More out of habit than because he felt unsteady, Frank kept his hand on the dog's harness.

Eli stood, looking from his mom at the front of the church to the back exit. Frank moved to where he and Dozer blocked the escape option.

Eli heaved a big sigh and trudged toward the front of the church. Frank waited until it was clear from body language that Eli was telling his mother what he'd done. Evelyn rushed up and started talking, no doubt filling in the details.

Frank turned and headed toward the exit.

Suddenly Fisk was walking beside him. They headed out of the church into a crisp, blue-sky day.

"How's April's ankle?" Frank asked his brother.

Fisk raised an eyebrow. "Surprised you don't know."

Frank didn't want to get into it, so he shrugged. "We didn't talk this morning."

"Okaaay," Fisk said. "Something wrong?"

"Nope." Frank watched a blue jay hop among the tree branches beside them.

They walked toward the street. "Looks like your vestibular stuff has gone away," Fisk said.

"My… Oh. You know, you're right. I haven't had a problem in more than a week." Then he shrugged. "The doctors warned me that it might come and go."

"Or it might go away entirely, right?"

"Right."

Fisk looked down at Dozer, plodding between them. "If it does go away," he said, "what will you do with Dozer?"

Frank's grip on the harness tightened. "Dozer's mine, no matter what." The dog had seen him through a hard time. And it seemed like there was a different kind of hard time coming, because he felt as low as dirt. Dozer's side hustle as an emotional support dog was about to become a full-time gig.

"You're loyal to the dog, but not to her?" Fisk gestured toward the church.

Frank pretended not to understand. "Who?"

Rolling his eyes, Fisk stopped and put a hand on Frank's forearm. "You know who. What happened?"

"You don't want to know," Frank said.

Fisk just stood there.

"She's still the same person she was," Frank said. "She's a cheater. I may be loyal, but I'm not one to make the same mistake twice."

Chapter Ten

A week and a half after the big blowup with Frank, April knocked on the door of a pretty farmhouse a couple miles out of town.

It was Wednesday, January 31, a cold, blustery day. April had finished the last bit of work she could do alone and emailed the whole document to Frank, so she had a little respite from the project...and from him.

Jodi, Cam's wife, opened the door. Her son JJ was in the twins' class, and Jodi had agreed to help April prepare for the Valentine's party, which was coming up all too soon. "Come in, come in, it's freezing out there," Jodi said. She ushered April into the house, took her coat and led her into the kitchen. Which smelled amazing.

"What are you making, muffins? Coffee cake?"

"Cookies," Jodi said. "You said you'd bring lunch, which you did *not* have to do, but since you did, I figured I'd supply dessert."

"Wonderful." April set the boxes of Chinese takeout at one end of the pine-plank table. She set her bag of craft supplies at the other end. "Do you want to eat first, or do our work?"

"Eat, for sure," Jodi said, laughing. "This is a treat for me. Nova, my four-year-old, has a playdate after preschool. So we have, like, three hours to visit and slam this party into shape. Hey, how's your ankle?"

"So much better." April flexed it and winced. "Still a little sore, and I'm not going on any long hikes for a couple of weeks, but I'm off crutches."

"Getting Frank and the twins to wait on you?"

Considering that she hadn't seen Frank for days, that wasn't a possibility. And the twins had been helpful at first, but now they were back to expecting Mom to be Mom. Which was fair, for a couple of six-year-olds. "They've been helpful," she said, keeping it vague.

"I'm sure," Jodi said with a snort. She set a pair of plates on the table. "Silverware or chopsticks?" she asked.

"I'm gonna say silverware. I'm too hungry to fumble around with chopsticks."

"Same," Jodi said.

As they scooped food onto their plates, April looked around the cozy kitchen. A big window over the sink let in daylight and provided a view of the backyard. Right now, the yard was wet and the trees bare, but it would be a wonderful place for kids to play come summer.

The kitchen itself was cheerfully retro. Each of the wooden chairs around the table was painted a different bright color. The cupboards were a pale green, and gingham curtains hung at the window. "I love what you've done with this place. I think I heard you just bought it?"

"We did. It's new to us, but not new." Jodi scooped orange chicken onto her plate of rice. "The house is from the 1950s, so we decided to go with that theme." She hesitated, biting her lip, and met April's eyes. "I know some of Cam's brothers think he was wrong to buy a house this big, but the truth is, we're expecting again."

"Oh, that's wonderful!" April jumped up and hugged Jodi. "You two seem like such great parents."

"We really wanted one more," Jodi said. "But...well, it looks like it might be two, not one."

"Twins?" April's eyes widened. "Oh, wow. You're going to have such a handful. And so much joy."

"Open to any advice you can offer," Jodi said. "But keep the news to yourself. We don't want to tell anyone until the first trimester's over."

"Of course." April sat down again and crunched into an egg roll. "I'm here for you if you have any twin-related questions. Although my situation was pretty different from…this." She waved a hand around the cozy kitchen.

Jodi sipped tea. "Different how? If you want to share."

April liked Jodi, and the warm kitchen seemed like a cozy refuge from the rest of the world. "Single mom, no money, no support, no friends."

"Oh, that sounds awful! How did you manage?"

"Honestly, I couldn't have made it without help from a church I started attending. That's when faith became more than a word to me. Those people…" Her throat tightened and tears sprang to her eyes. She fanned her face, trying to keep things at least a little light. "Sorry. It's just, they helped me find public assistance and a place to stay, and when the time came, two of the older women were there at my side throughout the whole delivery. It was really a blessing."

"I'm so glad you had help," Jodi said. "Those people were true Christians. But still...it couldn't have been easy."

"No, never easy. I wanted to get off public assistance as fast as I could, so I figured out that if I took a job at a child care center, the kids could come with me and have care for a really low rate. If I had to work overtime, they could stay. It was a good solution, but child care doesn't pay a lot. No room for frills. When the kids started needing extras, gifts for other kids' birthday parties, new clothes every few months in their growth spurts, that's when I started writing articles on the side."

"Well, I'm impressed," Jodi said. "You handled all of that so well. You must feel great about yourself."

Great about herself? That had never even occurred to her as a possibility. "Not hardly. I never feel like I'm doing a good enough job."

"That's motherhood, right?" Jodi sighed. "Guilt. All the time. If I spend a few hours working, I feel like I'm neglecting my kids. And if I play with the kids, I feel like I'm not doing my share to support the family."

"Wow. Even with all this, you feel that way?"

Jodi looked puzzled. "All *what*?"

April spread her hands. "A husband, a nice house, a good writing gig, lots of family and friends around you. It seems so perfect."

Jodi laughed. "It's far from perfect. *I'm* far from perfect. Just ask Cam or any of my kids." She pushed her plate away, looking thoughtful. "When I came back to Holiday Point, I was newly widowed from an abusive husband. The job I'd set up fell through at the last minute, and the only other possibility was working for the man who'd dumped me after two dates in high school."

222 The Veteran's Valentine Helper

"Cam?"

"Uh-huh. It took effort and help and counseling for both of us to get it together enough to have a relationship. We're still a work in progress."

"I guess everyone is. Thanks for telling me that."

"Of course!" Jodi smiled at her, and April felt a seed of happiness start to grow. It was good to have a friend. "I guess we should get started with this party prep."

"You're right. I got you into this, and I don't want it to take up your whole day."

Jodi waved a hand. "I'm happy to help. That survey you sent around to all the parents in the class was great. I assume there's a history?"

"There is." April carried her dishes to the sink. "The initial group of parent helpers couldn't agree on how the party should go. Darci Mae wanted a much fancier party, and I just had a hunch that other moms would feel like I did, that simple and home-made is better."

"Obviously you were right."

"Simple won by a landslide," April admitted. "And then Darci Mae and Lily quit."

"Because they couldn't get their way?" Jodi shook her head. "That's just stunningly ridiculous."

"To be fair," April said, "I don't think Lily wanted to, but she was afraid to go against Darci Mae."

Jodi paused in the middle of loading their plates into the dishwasher. "We should totally do a blog post on mom dynamics!"

April's jaw dropped. "That is *such* a good idea. We could do a whole book!"

"I would love to write a book with you," Jodi said, and then offered a rueful smile as her hand came to rest on her belly. "When we get some free time."

"Yeah. Let's revisit the idea when your twins are in school." April started pulling their craft supplies out of the bag, smiling. Red paper, pink paper, paper doilies in white.

Jodi brought scissors and glue to the table. "So what's our plan?"

"We need to cut out a gazillion hearts. Like, four hundred? Some are for the letter math game, and some are for musical hearts. Those should be bigger."

"On it." Jodi grabbed a pink stack and started folding paper in half. "So, how are things going with the book?"

That was the question of the year.

She'd typed up the notes she had from her talk with Frank, had listened to the recording a couple of times to make sure she got everything in.

It had almost killed her to do it.

Sitting there on the very couch where they'd kissed, listening to Frank describe a horrific and heroic chain of events in his understated way, had been a unique style of torture. The very sound of his voice had made her clench her jaw, knowing he thought the worst of her. But then she'd listen to a few more sentences and her heart would melt, because she admired what he'd done and liked the man he'd become.

Jodi paused in the middle of cutting out a pink paper heart. "Uh…we don't have to talk about the book. I totally get it if you don't want to. I mean, I've been pretty blocked before and people asking about your project just makes it worse. I'm sorry."

"No, it's fine. I'm not blocked or anything, it's just…" Should she tell Jodi what was going on? Normally she kept stuff like that to herself, but Jodi had shared about the twins she might be expecting. And about her difficult past. It might help April to talk to Jodi about the situation. "It's just that, well, I'm not speaking with Frank."

"Whoa whoa whoa. How can you write a book with someone you're not speaking to? How long has it been this way?"

April's scissors moved off line and cut her latest paper heart in half. She shoved the pieces away. "It's getting to the point where we have to talk. It's been a week and a half, and we've had our separate things to work on. Communicated by text for quick stuff, email for bigger issues."

"That sounds stressful."

"It has been. I keep waking up in the middle of the night worrying about it. Like whether we'll get the book done and in. I make half my pay for time put in, but the other half is linked to delivery and acceptance of the manuscript."

"Wow." Jodi's forehead wrinkled as she pulled another stack of construction paper toward her. "How come you took the job, if you don't mind my asking? I mean, I get that it's great to have a writing gig, here, but if you knew you and Frank had big issues…"

April shook her head. "His identity was masked for privacy and safety. We didn't know we'd be working together until we encountered each other face-to-face."

"For the first time since…"

"Seven years ago." She sighed. "We

thought we could work together, keep it impersonal, but…"

"But you both practically burst into flames when you're in the same room," Jodi said dryly.

April's eyes widened. "You saw that?"

"Sure did." Jodi smiled. "I have a good sense for those things."

April drew in a deep breath and let it out slowly. "What I'm trying to figure out is…can the kids and I build a life here, in Holiday Point? With Frank so close by, and with us at odds. I mean, I love it here—"

"Wait a sec." Jodi waved a pair of scissors at her. "You think you're like, permanently at odds?"

April thought about his almost offhand question: *Why'd you cheat?* He hadn't even sounded upset about it. He'd just sounded certain—like he'd *known* for a fact that she'd cheated.

Which, of course, she hadn't. He didn't know her at all.

If he came to realize the truth, if he came

to believe that he was the only one she'd slept with, then it would have to dawn on him that he was the twins' father.

"Does Frank suspect the twins are his?" Jodi's words were so quiet that they could have been a whisper in April's own head.

She stared at her new friend, her throat going dry. She swallowed hard. "You... you think they're Frank's?"

Jodi made an apologetic face. "I mean, it's just a guess. I figure it's for the two of you to work out. I haven't told a soul."

April met Jodi's sincere eyes and actually believed her. "I can't talk about their parentage because I need to tell him—tell the father—first."

"Of course. I'm here to support you if you need it." She frowned. "Like you said, you need to talk to him first. And I'd suggest you do it soon, because people are going to start doing the math if they haven't already."

April blew out a breath, a sick, scared

feeling spreading through her chest. "You're probably right."

"And you're not speaking to each other," Jodi said thoughtfully as she pushed aside another stack of hearts. "The Wilkins men have tempers, especially if they think they've been disrespected. That's the one area where their daddy comes out in all of them."

"I can see where thinking you'd been cheated on would spark up your temper," April said.

Jodi's eyebrows shot up. "He thinks that?"

"Yep. He's sure of it. No basis in fact, but…" She lifted her hands, palms up. "What do facts matter when your manhood is at stake?"

Jodi rolled her eyes, then pulled her knees to her chest and wrapped her arms around them, perched on the chair. "Men. You know, everyone's always wondered why Frank left and never came back. Mostly, people figured it was the Wilkins reputation he was running from. But I actually wonder if he was running from you."

"That makes no sense. Why would he run and hide from me?"

"If seeing you hurt too much. If he couldn't stop thinking about you and caring about you and wanting you."

"And then he thought I cheated." April used a thick marker to write letters on construction-paper hearts. "You're saying I hurt him."

Jodi shrugged. "Love hurts, right? I'm sure he hurt you, too, especially if…well. I don't know the sequence of events and it's not my business, but it sure sounds like the two of you have some talking to do. If you ever want to send the twins over so you can get a few hours to work things out together, I'm just a text away."

"Aw, thank you!" April hugged Jodi. It was so, so good to feel like she had a friend. Like there was someone here in Holiday Point who had her back.

She knew, of course, that God had her back. But it was nice to have a good girl-friend at your side, too.

Just get it done in the next two weeks and then working with her will be over.

Frank walked into the dining room they used as a shared office, determined to work hard, keep it impersonal and get it over with.

When he saw April's dark head bent over some handwritten notes, the impersonal goal went out the window. She was so serious and capable and cute, jeans-clad legs wrapped around the legs of her chair, elbows propped on the table.

He cleared his throat. "Uh…good morning. How do you want to get started?"

His words seemed to jolt her. When she looked up, there was something dark and vulnerable in her eyes. Quickly, it was gone. She reached out a hand to Dozer, who'd walked in beside Frank, and rubbed the big dog's head. "The only way I've ever approached this stage is to spread the pages out on the table and go through them together. Can you do that?"

Her tone implied that he couldn't. That maybe he'd go all emotional and freak out.

He could be as professional as she could. He put his bag down on his desk with an extra-loud thump. "Sure."

"You have your notes printed out, right?"

"On my tablet." He held it up. When she'd suggested this meeting, she'd asked that he print out the notes, but he felt like he was doing a lot just being here. He'd rather read his notes off the tablet computer. "Is that a problem?"

She started putting pages on the table, making rows. "For me, paper is better, but you do you."

Dozer flopped to the floor, back end first, front end thumping down hard. He let out a long sigh and put his head on his paws.

Frank felt like sighing, too, as he sat down at his desk and rolled up his sleeves and found the right section on his computer. There was no small talk, no *How was your weekend?* or *How are the kids?* It was silent, awkwardly so.

Once they started working, the awkwardness continued. They both had to lean over the pages to look at them, which meant standing close together, sometimes bumping into each other. They both reacted lightning-fast to any such contact, jumping back, apologizing.

Still, they had to talk it through and he felt obligated to give her well-deserved praise. She'd put his disjointed notes and halting interview together and made a story. "That part worked with almost no changes. You're very talented."

Her cheeks went pink and a smile flashed across her face, quickly stifled. "Thanks. I'm glad it's working. But what about this section?" She pointed at a part where details were lacking, and then they were off, with both of them taking fast and furious notes, him on his keyboard and her on an old-fashioned oblong pad of paper.

The third or fourth time they touched accidentally and then jerked away from each other, Frank had had enough. "Do you want to talk about the...the *thing* that happened last week?"

Again her cheeks went pink, and Frank could have kicked himself for liking the look on her. He had to stay away from a woman who didn't share his values about monogamy.

"No, I don't want to talk about it," she said, speaking to the table instead of to him. "We agreed to wait until the book's done, remember? After that, we can." Her gaze flickered up to his and back down again. "If you want."

"Okay." Her words and posture made him want to protect her. Her whole demeanor was at odds with a cheater.

But that was exactly why he had to exercise extreme caution. She was a great actor, but her sweetness wasn't real.

His emotions threatened to overwhelm him. He wanted to leave. *Compartmentalize*, he ordered himself. He finally managed to get the soft, hurt side of his heart sectioned off again so he could focus on the business at hand. They worked rapidly and well together, but after another hour April stepped back and shook her head. "Something's missing."

"Okay…" Frank waited. He didn't trust *her*, but he trusted her instincts as a writer.

She reviewed what they'd written, going back over a section twice, then one more time. "It's not engaging enough. We need details. Site details, sensory details."

"I tried. I'm not gonna remember much more." He lifted his hands, palms up. "I wasn't focused on smelling the roses at the time."

"No, of course not. You were focused on the mission. But to put the reader in the scene, we need to give it more color." She looked up at him. "Could we… I mean, is it possible for us to take a trip down there?

Maybe even set up an interview with that boy you saved?"

Frank's heart kicked, hard. An instant layer of sweat formed on his forehead, and he used his sleeve to brush it away.

See Elijah Lee, talk to him again after all these months? What if the boy was doing poorly, if he hadn't recovered from the losses he'd experienced? Frank had sent money to Elijah Lee's grandmother, faithfully each month, but he'd had plenty of excuses to put off a visit.

The truth was, he didn't know if he could handle it.

Dozer came over and leaned against Frank's leg.

And then there was the idea of traveling with April. The trip to Meekersville was two hours, three if there was weather. It could be done in a day if pushed, but that was a long time to spend together.

"Bad idea?" Her tone was light, but forced.

"Yeah. Maybe. I don't know." He was

trying not to resist, to be open to her suggestions, to let the bad feelings inside him come to the surface so they could be released. And so the book would be good and do its job. "Let's think on it."

"Sure," she said, "but if we're going to do it, it needs to be within the next week so we'll have a few days to incorporate any details we want to add. The deadline's coming."

"I know, I know." He stepped back from the table and was suddenly dizzy. He reached for Dozer and steadied himself.

It was the first time in a week he'd felt the vertigo. He'd thought, or hoped at least, that it was over with.

Jodi's phone buzzed. She leaned over and looked at it, then picked it up. "Sorry, I have to take this. It's the school." She took the call and listened, her eyes widening. "Oh, no! Is the other boy okay?"

She listened again, hunching away from him. "Of course. I'll be right down." She ended the call and spun to face him.

"What ha—"

"Eli hit another boy. They may suspend him! I'm partly blaming you."

"What?"

She marched out of the office and headed toward the front door. He followed her as she grabbed her coat and shrugged into it.

"It would have been better if he'd never thought about how to react to a bully. At least when he cried and hid, he wasn't hurting anyone!"

Frank blew out a breath. There was so much wrong with what she'd just said, but it was true that Eli had changed his tune because of Frank's advice. Uneasily, he thought of Eli getting into a conflict with another boy in Sunday school last week.

Maybe Frank hadn't made things clear enough. Obviously he hadn't, if the kid was getting kicked out of school.

"She said the other family is threatening a lawsuit!" Her voice rose and broke on the last words. "I can't afford a lawsuit. What am I going to do?"

"Eli can't have done much damage," Frank said, trying to be soothing. "He's just a little guy, and he has a good heart."

"He *used* to," she said, biting her lip. "I didn't mean to blame you. It's my responsibility how they're raised." She sounded choked up, like she was about to cry.

He grabbed his own coat and the keys to his truck. "Come on," he said. "I'll drive you. And I'm coming in."

"You can drive me, but you can't come in," she said. "I don't need to have you and Eli high-fiving each other. I have to smooth this over."

"I promise, I won't encourage it."

"Olivia said he was defending Evelyn, and Evelyn was defending another kid, a little guy with a disability. A boy named Bentley was teasing him at recess. Evelyn stepped in, and then Eli."

A little surge of pride rose up in Frank, but he tamped it down. "He needs to learn to go to the authorities in the school, not take care of problems himself."

"Will you say that to him? I have a feeling it'll go over better coming from you than from his mom." He was glad to see she sounded better, less upset. "The mom is Darci Mae. Bentley is that kid who was over here a few weeks ago."

"Whoa. Is this going to turn into a mom war?"

She spun on him. "That's just like a man to make light of an argument because it's women. That mom could destroy my opportunities in this town, if the gossip goes against me."

"Hey." He held the truck door for her. "I get it. I'm a Wilkins. I know how the gossip circuit can hurt you."

She looked stricken. "That's true, you do. I'm sorry. I'm just… I really want things to go well for us in Holiday Point. I love being back here. I want to stay, if…if it can all work out."

Frank could fill in the blanks. *If* they

succeeded in completing this job. And *if* she found another job and place to live once this was done. She'd mentioned applying for several jobs, but since they'd been at odds, he didn't know whether she'd gotten any interviews.

Well, he didn't trust her, but he felt for her. He made a promise to himself. They'd get the book done, and if gossip went against her, he'd enlist his brothers and their wives in making it right. Just by virtue of being a big family, and because they'd all turned their lives around, they had some influence here.

She still looked tense, and he knew he couldn't fix it, but there was one more thing he could do. He put on his signal and turned into the school parking lot. "I'll help you make this right with Eli, if I can," he said. "And then if we can figure out the logistics, I'm willing to do a quick trip to West Virginia."

Her face lit up. "Really?" Of course, she

immediately looked at the school and got all serious and worried again.

Oh, man, did he ever want to pull her into his arms.

Chapter Eleven

"I still don't think I should have let Eli go today," April said. She adjusted her seat belt. It was Sunday morning. They were in Frank's truck, headed south, having just left the twins with Cam and Jodi. Dozer rode along in the back seat. "Going to a water park is a treat, and after what he did, he doesn't deserve a treat."

Frank slowed for an icy section, then sped up again. "I agree, he shouldn't have hit the kid, but he didn't do it out of the blue. And we talked to him about making a different choice next time."

"He was grounded all day yesterday. I

did make him do extra chores last night, and skip his favorite show." April was trying to convince herself she'd done the right thing. "But still…"

"He's a fine boy, and you're teaching him right from wrong. It'll be okay." Frank reached over and patted her arm, then pulled his hand back quickly.

They were on better terms, but not arm-patting terms. Frank had been great, driving her to the school and discussing the situation seriously with Eli. Eli had cried and apologized to the other boy by phone, and it looked like there wasn't going to be a lawsuit as Darci Mae had threatened.

As for apologies, Frank had apologized to her for giving Eli the wrong message. He'd admitted he didn't know enough about kids to understand how Eli might have perceived his teachings about bullying.

Even April, who hated the thought of her little boy doing anything rough or violent, had to admit that this was a complicated case. According to the twins' teacher, Olivia, Bentley had been teasing and pushing another child who had a disability, and Evelyn had defended him. Bentley had shoved Evelyn away, at which point Eli had rushed in like an avenging superhero. Yes, he'd hit Bentley, but he'd wanted to protect his twin.

When Jodi had called with a last-minute invite for the twins to join their family and a couple of cousins to spend the day at an indoor water park, April couldn't say no. How many times would she have a free Sunday, and just when she needed it, to go with Frank on this trip to revisit his West Virginia past?

As they drove, the ominous clouds that had hung over their part of the mountains cleared away, and spots of blue sky started to appear. Frank turned on the radio, and with both of them singing along—badly— to the latest country hits, the trip went quickly.

Within two hours, they'd pulled into the

small city of Meekersville, where Frank had worked on his last drug operation. Although a bit run-down, the place didn't look bad: the downtown was lively with people shopping, and the county courthouse looked pretty with a snow-covered lawn. Little houses lined the residential neighborhoods they drove through, and kids played outside.

She said as much to Frank.

"You're right," he said as he turned a corner, steering them through the town with an air of close familiarity. "It's a beautiful little town, or it once was. Beautiful country."

"Did you live here?" she asked, curious.

"Nearby, and I spent a lot of time here, undercover. It's my kind of place. Like home, without the Wilkins reputation." He paused, then added, "Except for the fact that it has the worst drug problem in the tri-state area."

"That still surprises me." They'd talked about it briefly while working on the book. Now she put down her notes and looked around, marveling that anything dark could lie beneath the charming look of the town.

"Uh-huh. Let me give you the cop tour." He proceeded to drive them through the same streets, but this time, he pointed out a shabby Victorian. "See that house? Belongs to a dealer. There's probably eight or ten addicts passed out in there. Passed out or worse."

"In a regular neighborhood?" She'd seen what they used to call crack houses, but they tended to be in vacant, burned-out parts of bigger cities.

He nodded and they drove on. "That group by the statue? Trouble."

They just looked like teenagers to April, maybe a little shaggier than most. But she believed him, especially when he said, "I understand from Elijah Lee's grandma that he got caught up with them for a little while."

"It's hard to get out, isn't it?"

"Yep. And that's why Elijah Lee and his grandma moved to another part of town. He goes to a private religious school there, and she said they like the neighborhood better, too. More room for a garden."

Why did she get the feeling he'd been involved with their move, facilitated it? "Do you think things have gotten any better since you... Since what happened?"

"I do. To a degree."

When they visited the block where the shoot-out had taken place, Frank got quiet. April walked around, dictating notes into her phone, trying to capture the sights and sounds and smells of the area. She wanted to portray it vividly and accurately.

After an hour, they left. Frank's jaw was clenched, his hands on the steering wheel tight.

"It's hard for you to come back here, where you were injured," she guessed. She didn't want to intrude or pry, but if possible, she needed to know how this visit was landing with him. It was good material for the book.

He looked straight ahead. The windshield wipers swished back and forth, clearing slush and cold rain. "I miss being a cop. I liked the work."

Although his tone was matter-of-fact, pain lurked behind the stoic facade. April could hear it in his voice, see it in the set of his chin.

It made her think. And then she pulled out her phone and started tapping notes, a new angle for the end of the book. Drugs changed everyone's life, the addicts, the dealers, the families, the kids…but also the cops. Frank's chosen career had been taken from him in one moment.

He parallel-parked the truck beside a town park. Though small, it was lit with quaint lampposts and centered around a gazebo. Charming. But what did it hide?

"Wait, I'll come around," he ordered. He and Dozer circled the truck. Frank opened the door and helped her down.

A shadow darted from one tree to the next, getting closer. "Frank," she said. "To your right. By the benches now."

"Are you Mr. Frank?" The voice sounded younger than the kid's lanky height had initially suggested.

"I sure am," he said. "Elijah Lee. You've grown a foot since I last saw you." When the boy approached, Frank reached out and shook his hand.

The boy's grin was broad. "You came to see me! And you brought a dog!" He knelt down and started petting Dozer, ignoring the service vest.

Frank didn't correct the boy. He just ducked his head, and April saw a trace of his emotional reaction to coming here.

"My gram's sitting on the bench right there." The boy gestured for them to follow him. As they approached, an older lady stood. She was slender, a faded blonde, with fine wrinkles fanning out from pale blue eyes.

She reached out both hands to Frank.

"Thank you again, sir, for saving my boy. And for sending money every month. You don't have to do that."

He lifted one shoulder in a quick shrug. "I can. Hope it helps." He looked sharply at Elijah Lee. "You being good, taking care of your gram?"

"Yes, sir," the boy said.

As he took off his hat, April saw the scar that passed down one side of his scalp.

Frank and Elijah Lee walked off toward the pavilion, talking, the shorter boy looking up at the big man, Dozer on Frank's other side. April snapped a couple of quick pictures. "I can delete if you want, or just send them to you," she said to Elijah Lee's grandma. "Or if you wouldn't mind signing a release, they might get into the book we're working on. If you and Frank decide that's the right thing to do. I'd need a release from you, too, because I'd like to take a few shots of you and Elijah Lee."

"Whatever you need, honey," the woman said, looking pleased. She filled out the forms April had brought, and then they leaned against the car, their breath making clouds in the cold air, waiting for Frank and Elijah Lee to finish talking.

"You're raising him?" April asked.

"Yes. I was partly doing that even before his mother passed." The older woman looked away, staring out over the snowy streets. Then she looked back at April. "It fell to me, and I'm glad to do it. You take care of your own." She looked at April more sharply. "You Frank's woman?"

"No," April said quickly. "We're working together on the book, that's all."

"He's a good man."

"He is." April mostly believed that.

And as they said goodbye and got into the truck and headed back to Holiday Point, April battled with herself.

Frank *was* a good man. She'd seen more evidence of it on this visit. She needed to tell him the truth.

"Whew, that was emotional," Frank admitted as he navigated the winding mountain road, made slick by the freezing rain that was starting to come down. "But good."

"We can talk about what it meant to you, but for now, I'll let you focus on the road."

"Good. Gives me time to process." He flashed a smile.

Relief washed over her. She didn't have to tell him. Shouldn't. Couldn't, really, when he was driving in dangerous conditions.

She'd gotten a reprieve, but she couldn't let it be a long one. Frank deserved to know, and the twins deserved a father.

Frank's hands tightened on the steering wheel as he guided the car around another nearly hairpin curve. His tires slid briefly but the antilock brakes helped him stay in control. His headlights illuminated the steady, wet snowfall, big flakes melting on the windshield.

A car behind them sped up and passed

them on the straightaway, its taillights fading in the distance.

Frank restrained the brief urge to speed up and chase it. "Wise guy," he said. "Passing in these conditions."

"Perfect mix of rain and snow," April said as she pulled out her phone and studied the face of it. "My weather app says it's thirty-three degrees."

"And dropping, right?"

"Says so. There's a winter weather advisory now."

It could be he'd made a mistake driving out in these conditions. A more cautious man would have grabbed a couple of hotel rooms and hunkered down for the night. But Frank was wired to take charge and make decisions, and when she'd said she wanted to get home to her kids, that had made priorities clear in his mind.

His mission was to get this mom home to her kids. And secondarily, but still important, to get both of them home to finish the book by the end of the week.

And after that, what? April had said she wanted to stay in the area, and Frank was pretty sure he did, too. Would they follow up on this attraction and get together? Did he want that?

She hadn't apologized for cheating. In fact, she'd acted insulted that he'd even suggest the idea.

Could he be wrong?

His father wasn't the most reliable source, but he'd been so adamant, and Mom had backed him up. So had a friend who'd hung around with them that summer. But when he thought about it, that guy had wanted to date April himself and had been bitter that she'd chosen Frank.

A battle raged inside him. His soldier side thought in black-and-white and would cut her cold. His emotional side, which he'd started to value only after nearly losing his life, wanted to give her another chance. Ethically, she didn't deserve one. But he was a Christian, and a good Christian would forgive and forget.

A forgiving man was likely to get stomped in the real world. His childhood, his military training and his inner cop all shouted that conclusion.

But when he thought about his brothers, it seemed to him they'd all learned to bend a little, to open up, and yes, to forgive.

They were coming up on a pair of taillights, and Frank braked carefully.

"Is it stopped, or just going slow?" April squinted through the windshield. "I think it's moving."

Frank wondered if it was the car that had passed them earlier. He braked harder. The downhill grade didn't help.

The car in front of them started fishtailing and then spun.

"He's going off the road!" April gripped the dashboard, leaning forward.

That could have gone very, very bad if the car had spun toward the overhang, but it veered back toward the cliff side and stopped, mostly off the road.

Frank eased to a stop in a slightly wider

area behind the sedan and put on his flashers. "Flares in the back," he said. "Know how to use them?"

"Yes." She checked behind them and then got out of the truck.

Frank jogged up to the disabled car and discovered a man of about his own age, sitting in the driver's seat, looking disoriented. "Are you all right, sir?" he asked.

The man looked over at Frank and frowned as if he were having trouble processing the words. He shifted his neck from one side to the other.

"Turn off the vehicle," Frank ordered, and the man did so. "I'm going to call emergency services," Frank said. Not only did they need to get this car all the way off the road, but this guy kept rubbing at his chest. Could be bruising from the seat belt, but it could also be something more serious, like his heart. His coloring was bad, too. Frank reached an operator and made a report, and with the help of GPS she was able to locate their precise location.

"Ambulance on the way," he told the guy. "Why don't you come back and sit in my car, if you're able to move?" He wouldn't have asked it, but the back of the man's car extended out into the road. If someone missed the flares... And speaking of that, he needed to make sure April was off the road.

He looked up and she was jogging toward them, and Frank felt a flash of the same feeling he'd gotten around his army brothers. It was good to be with someone who had your back and was calm in an emergency. You pretty much learned that in the military. April had never served, but maybe raising twins alone had taught her how to handle a crisis.

Regardless of how she'd come by it, he liked it.

The man in the car leaned back against the headrest and closed his eyes.

"Sir? You need to stay awake. Can you get out of the car?"

April reached his side. "Is he okay?" she asked quietly.

"Not sure." Frank shook his head a little, so only April could see. He didn't want to scare the guy, but he definitely needed medical attention.

The man tried to twist in the seat and winced. "Peaches. Is she okay?"

"There's someone else back there?" Frank tried to peer around the man.

April scratched ice off the back window. "It's a dog!"

"In some kind of carrier seat?" Frank asked, and April nodded. "Looks like it." Good. The animal could have been hurt or killed otherwise.

A vehicle with flashing lights pulled up directly behind the sedan. A paramedic in a heavy coat emerged from the passenger side and jogged toward them. Within minutes she and her partner had gotten the man out of the car and into the back of the ambulance. "It's a good thing we were nearby on another call," she said. "Otherwise, out here on a night like this, you could have been waiting an hour or more."

April walked alongside the stretcher while Frank pulled the car all the way off the road. Once it was as safe as he could make it in these conditions, he put on the emergency flashers, turned off the car and then twisted to look in the back seat.

A small brown-and-white dog—what were they called, King Cavalier or something?—sat in a dog seat in the back, trembling, big brown eyes entreating. It didn't let out a single yip.

"Hey, little lady, you'll be okay. We'll figure out what to do with you." After some fumbling, he managed to get the carrier out of the rear seat. He carried it toward his car, but April called out to him. "Bring the dog here!"

He changed directions and went to the ambulance.

"Sir, we can't take the dog," one of the paramedics said. "We can notify the police that they'll need to take it to a shelter when they deal with your car."

"Not a shelter!" The man fumbled for his phone, unlocked it and handed it to April. "Call my brother, he's under 'Bro.' Tell him to come get Peaches. Please."

"Of course we will," she reassured him. "Peaches will be fine. You focus on getting well." She placed a quick phone call and then returned the phone to the man. "Your brother will be here shortly. It's fine for you to go."

The man sank back on the stretcher, and moments later the ambulance sped off.

"Are you up for waiting on this road a little while?" she asked.

Still holding Peaches in her carrier, Frank looked up at the sky, raining snow. Kicked at the slushy ice that was starting to accumulate on the road. "We can wait a bit," he said. "If the brother can't get here quickly, we'll have to take Peaches with us. I don't want to get us stuck out here in the snow." And this was why he should have been more cautious. Yes, he was a good driver on snow, but you had to consider that other people might not be. When things didn't go as planned, what had been a slight risk became a bigger one.

Live and learn. "I'm sorry I brought us out in this weather," he said. "Too risky."

She was texting. "He says he can be here in twenty minutes. Knows where it is and has four-wheel drive. He'll take Peaches and let the rest of the family know what happened."

"Okay." He turned back toward the truck. "Come on. We may as well wait where it's warm and dry."

They walked toward the truck. A few steps away from it, she put a hand on his arm. "Wait."

He stopped, and realized there was utter silence. No other cars on the road, everything muffled in a coating of snow, now falling softly around them. When he breathed in, there was the slightly metallic smell of the snow mixed with the heady scent of evergreens that surrounded them.

"It's breathtaking," she whispered. She closed her eyes and lifted her face to the snow.

It looked like she was praying. But praying was far from Frank's mind. He wanted to hold her in his arms, to kiss that up-turned face.

From inside the truck, Dozer let out a deep "woof."

"We'd better let Dozer know we're all safe," April said. "Will he get along with Peaches?"

"Since they're both restrained, it's not a disaster if they don't make friends." He opened the truck's back door and leaned in. "Got a girlfriend for you, buddy," he said, and eased the carrier onto the back seat beside Dozer, who was harnessed in on the other side.

Dozer woofed again.

Peaches found her voice and let out a couple of strong, defensive yaps.

Dozer leaned closer and sniffed her, and realizing it was all going to be fine, Frank helped April into the truck and climbed in himself.

"Awww, he likes her," April said. She was on her knees, looking into the back seat, where Dozer had nosed his way into the top of the carrier and was licking Peaches's head.

They watched the dogs for a few minutes and then settled into their seats. Frank was still very aware of that desire to hold April. Containing that overrode any ability he had to start a conversation. He turned on the radio, oldies at a low volume, then looked at her. "Rather have it quiet?" he asked.

"I would." She smiled at him as he turned off the radio. "As the mother of twins, quiet is something I don't experience very often, and it's *so* quiet here." She lowered her window a little, and that fresh snowy scent blew in on a gust of cold wind.

He slowed his breath and leaned against the headrest. "Lots of stars beyond those snow clouds," he said.

"All of it makes you feel small. Me, anyway."

"Me, too. Which is kind of a comfort. Reminds me I'm not in charge."

She laughed. "You always did like to be in charge." She pulled her knees to her chest, slipping her feet out of her fuzzy boots. Her socks were striped, wild shades of pink and orange and green.

"Cute," he said, gesturing toward them.

"A gift from the twins. One of the elves at the Christmas Market helped them. They're nice and warm."

She'd said her church had helped her, and he was guessing they'd helped with things like taking the twins Christmas shopping.

She looked over at him. "Most of us in Holiday Point grew up going to church, but I know my faith deepened when I needed to rely on God as a single mom," she said. "When did yours? Because I don't remember you talking much about God when we, um, dated before."

He thought about diving into a discussion of their earlier relationship. But they were stuck in a truck for who knew how long together, so he took the safer route. "I'm a cliché," he said. "Battlefield conversion. Plus, mine was under the stars in the desert."

"Don't make light of it," she said. "Whatever brings you closer to God is a good thing. My faith has gotten me through a lot of rough days. Not just the big stuff, but when the kids are squabbling or money's tight. Knowing He's right there with me makes things so much better."

"You're right." He stared out into the snow-dotted blackness. "When they thought I wouldn't make it, and then when my vertigo was making me sick all the time, the only thing to do was pray."

"I did a lot of praying, too. Still do, but when I was pregnant and alone in a strange city, it was pretty much continuous. I read my Bible and I prayed."

Again, Frank felt an inner battle. Sympathy for what she'd been through warred with his inner judgmental side pointing out that she'd brought it on herself. "Wouldn't the babies' father help you?"

She was quiet for a long moment. Then she spoke. "Frank. I have something to tell you."

His chest tightened as he looked at her serious face. He wasn't sure he wanted to hear whatever it was she had to say.

Chapter Twelve

❧

April looked into Frank's eyes, those eyes she'd fallen in love with as a teenager, warm with humor and understanding back then, now a deeper shade that reflected the depth of experience he'd gained since they'd first been together.

Her heart pounded rapidly. Her chest and neck felt warm.

He's the father of your kids. You have to tell him.

The sound of an approaching vehicle broke the silence. Headlights appeared through the falling snow, and then a truck pulled in behind them.

Peaches barked.

April drew in a breath and let it out slowly. She couldn't blurt it out now and expect them both to hold a conversation with a stranger immediately after.

She felt a little relief, but mostly frustration. She needed to tell him, and as time passed, she wanted to tell him.

He'd matured into a thoughtful, kind man. He'd understand why she'd kept the secret, once he got over the shock. How would he react? Was it possible he'd be happy about it?

Maybe he'd want to build something together, the two of them and the twins.

A large man climbed out of the truck and approached them.

Frank opened the truck door and got out, and April leaned over. Snow and cold air blew in, making her shiver.

The man greeted them, but immediately looked past them into the truck. "Where is she?"

April reached back and lifted the small

dog into the front seat, and she let out a couple more yips when she spotted the man.

"There you are," he said in a falsetto at odds with his tall, wide frame. "There's my little Peachie-boo."

Peaches's entire body wiggled with how hard she was wagging her tail.

Carefully, April handed her over. The man cuddled her in his arms, and she licked his heavily bearded face.

"No question she knows you," Frank said, laughing. "As far as your brother, he didn't seem badly injured, but since he kept rubbing his chest—"

"Him." The man waved a hand. "I *told* him not to take Peaches out in this weather, didn't I?" He held up the little dog and kissed its nose.

Frank glanced at April, the corners of his mouth twitching.

"They were taking your brother to Valley General," she said. "In addition to checking out his heart, they wanted to check for a head injury, since he seemed a little dazed."

"He'll be fine, hard as his head is." The man tucked Peaches inside his jacket, so that just her little face peeked out.

Frank raised an eyebrow. "Head injuries are nothing to take lightly."

"Oh, sure." The mountain man seemed to come out of his reverie of adoring Peaches. "Y'all better get moving, unless you want to spend the night here. Which you're welcome to. My house is ten minutes away, fifteen in this snow. Supposed to get worse out."

April got the dog seat out and handed it to the man, then bit her lip and looked at Frank. "I need to get home to the kids if we can."

"We can. Let's go."

After making sure Peaches and her adoring owner were safely in their truck, they pulled out and headed the rest of the way to Holiday Point.

The roads were too dangerous for April

to bring up any difficult topics. That would have to wait a little while longer.

The next morning, April woke up when bright sunshine came into her bedroom. She sat up, stretched and smiled. Nothing like total exhaustion to produce a sound night's sleep.

Fortunately, the twins had been exhausted, too, from their fun day with Hector and JJ. She and Frank had swung by and picked them up, and they'd all gone to bed immediately after arriving home.

April grabbed her phone and checked her notifications. School was canceled for the day, which was what everyone had been predicting last night. She hurried to the window and saw what looked like two feet of snow. The sun was already making the icicles that lined her windows drip.

It was so, so beautiful. She thought of the gray slush and cranky drivers they'd have faced in their city life, and lifted her face, thanking God for the beauty of His earth and for the opportunity He'd placed in their path.

As she dressed, she thought about Frank. They were so close to finished with the book, especially now that they'd done the West Virginia visit. It was time to tell him the truth about his children.

If only she could have told him last night. She'd felt so close to him, spiritually as well as emotionally, sitting in his truck on a dark, snowy mountain. He'd been relaxed, receptive, thoughtful.

When she thought about uttering the words now, in the light of day, her stomach knotted. He might be upset or angry, especially at first. She was confident he was a good man, but this would be a shock. Most people didn't like shocks that changed their entire lives, not at first.

And they were all snowed in together. If he got upset, the kids would know. She didn't want the truth to come out to Frank and the twins simultaneously. She wanted to tell him first. Once she saw how he reacted, maybe gave him a little time to get used to the idea, she'd work with him to figure out how and when to tell the twins.

As she looked out the window, she formulated a plan. She'd make sure they had a sweet, memorable day together. Both Frank and the twins could remember it as a family day, before they knew they were family.

She texted Frank.

Making pancakes. Come on down.

And then she heard stirring from the twins' rooms and opened both doors. "Snow day!" she called. "Wash your faces, and then come down in your PJs for breakfast."

After making sure both were up and smiling, she trotted down the stairs. Maybe it was the sunshine that was making her feel like singing.

But she knew better.

The idea of a family day for her and

Frank and the kids had brought on a wave of joy and longing. She wanted to have that full-time. She wanted to have a family, a husband and kids, and live with them, make a home for them. Not just any old family, either. She wanted Frank and the twins. She'd have chosen those three, exactly. That was God's way. His hand had been guiding her, all this time, toward her perfect happy ending.

At least, she hoped it would be a happy ending.

She started the pancakes, and in no time the four of them were around the table, enjoying a lazy meal. Dozer lay beside Frank, head on paws, eyes wide open as he watched for spills and crumbs.

"You kids need to play quietly while Mr. Frank and I work for a couple of hours," she told the twins. She and Frank had agreed last night, during the drive, to spend a couple of hours working with the information they'd gotten on yesterday's trip while it was fresh in their minds.

"Can we watch TV?" Evelyn asked.

"Yes, on the channels you always watch."

"Can we make a snowman after?" Eli asked.

She smiled. "Of course we can."

"Can *he* help?" Eli whispered to April, the words clearly audible to everyone at the table. He pointed at Frank.

She glanced at Frank, her cheeks going pink. She wanted him to help, too. "We'll have to see," she said.

He was drinking coffee, and his twinkling eyes met hers over the rim of the cup.

"Can you?" Evelyn begged.

"Please?" Eli added his voice. "We'll do the hard work."

Frank laughed. "Like your mom said, we'll have to see."

His eyes met hers again, and they both smiled.

Frank cleaned up the breakfast dishes while April got the children started on a puzzle they'd borrowed from the library. Hopefully that, plus some coloring pages and a new box of crayons, would keep them busy at the table for a while. April put on some music they liked, and then she and Frank headed into the adjoining office and got to work.

Something had shifted in their relationship during their trip to West Virginia, when Frank had shared more of his experiences and they'd struggled through that harrowing drive together. They laughed more often. When his hand brushed her shoulder as he leaned over her computer, she didn't flinch away.

She felt excited about what the future might hold, as excited as she had when she'd gotten her first article accepted at a major parenting magazine. No, more than that. She felt the same kind of nervous anticipation as when she'd held the twins in her arms for the first time. Then, she'd wondered: What would life hold for them as a family?

Now, she wondered the same thing about herself, the twins and Frank.

It was wrong of her to think about a future with Frank that way. She didn't know whether he could be depended upon for the long run. He'd left her before, and she had to get him to talk that through before taking a chance on him again.

Knowing how much they'd have to work out, how many different ways it could go, should make her pull away. She should act cool and proper, avoid giving him any ideas. But she'd loved Frank once. In fact, he was the only man she'd ever loved. And now, being around him, her feelings were blooming like flowers after a spring rain. No one else could come close to making her feel the way Frank made her feel.

An impossible mix of feelings warred in her: the desire to pursue the relationship no matter what, and the cautious mom, protective of herself and especially of her kids.

So the next time their hands brushed, and their eyes caught, she turned away, saved her document and stood. "I'm getting a little stir-crazy," she said, "and I'd like to get the kids outside for a little bit. Mind if we take a break?"

"Not if I can join you." He stacked their notes neatly. "I'm thinking the snow is perfect for packing. And Dozer needs to get outside and play. He loves the snow."

So they bundled up the kids and went outside. The snow was melting in the brilliant sunshine, but beneath the icy crust on top lay snow that made perfect giant snowballs. All four of them worked together, rolling and stacking snowballs for a little family of snowmen. Dozer ran in circles around them, tongue lolling out, before plopping down in the snow to rest.

April went inside for carrots and chocolate sandwich cookies to use as noses and eyes. When she looked out the kitchen window, Frank was holding Eli up to put a hat on the biggest snowman, while Evelyn stood back, gesturing, obviously telling them the proper way to angle it.

April's breath caught. *This*, she thought. This *is what I want. For them and for me.*

They went for a hike in the woods. Frank left Dozer out of his vest, and the dog seemed ecstatic, following trails of forest creatures and chasing sticks Frank threw. Frank was a good woodsman, showing the twins signs of rabbits and deer.

They crossed an icy stream and hiked up the next hill, and then abruptly, both twins got tired. Evelyn plopped down in the snow, and Eli rubbed his eyes with the backs of his hands.

If she were alone, April would have had to rouse them up and pep-talk them into making it home on their own steam. No way could she carry both of them. But Frank was there, swinging Evelyn up into his arms, leaving the lighter Eli for April to carry. He pointed out blue jays and nuthatches and a small woodpecker, and the novelty of what he had to say kept the twins from getting too cranky. Soon they were back at the house.

"A quick snack, and then a nap, I think," April said. They all sat down at the kitchen table and ate sandwiches as fast as April could make them. The twins revived enough to refuse the nap, so April got out craft supplies. "It's as good a time as any to make a valentines box," she said.

"Will you help?" Eli asked Frank.

"I don't know if I'll be much help," he said. "I've never made one before."

"Didn't you have valentines in the olden days?" Evelyn asked.

One corner of Frank's mouth rose. "It *was* a really long time ago," he said. "We had valentines, but I don't think my brothers and I made boxes at home."

"I'll show you how," Evelyn said importantly, and she took on directorship of the craft while April cleaned up their lunch dishes, threw together some cookie dough and put a tray of chocolate chip cookies into the oven.

"Will this win a prize at the Valentine's party?" Evelyn asked. She was holding up her box, with garish multicolored hearts and crooked stick figures. It was considerably less polished than the one Eli was working on.

"No prizes," April said quickly, forestalling a possibly tactless comment Eli had been about to make. "Everyone's making their own box, just how they want it. Yours has your favorite colors, and you drew our family on it. I'd know this was an Evelyn box even without your name."

"Would you know mine, Mom?" Eli asked. He held up his box, which sported a slightly Van Gogh–like sun and sky, along with heart-shaped flowers.

"I would," April said, smiling at her talented son. "I love both of them, and I know you'll get a lot of valentines." She knew it because she'd checked with Olivia. Every child was asked to bring a valentine for every other child. If money was short, there were discreet discount-store packages of them handed to kids or moms at pickup. No kid should be left out of the valentines exchange for lack of money or access to a store.

April pulled the cookies out of the oven and started moving them onto the counter, where paper towel–covered newspapers served as a cooling rack. Frank listened while Eli explained each drawing on his box and lifted Evelyn up so she could reach a new bottle of glue from a high shelf.

April wondered just how long this family scene could go on.

Another five minutes? Forever?

She was contemplating that when there was a loud pounding at the door.

It took a few seconds for Frank to recognize the bundled-up man at the door. When he did, he squinted to be sure. "Dad? What are you doing here?"

"Came to see if you all need anything," he said. He held out a bag of what looked like groceries.

"You didn't need to do that, Mr. Wilkins." April had come up behind him. "Come right on in. It's too cold for you to be out. Did you drive?" She helped his dad out of his thick green work jacket and handed it to Frank. "Come right on in and sit down."

She guided Frank's father to the kitchen table with a light arm around his back. Frank hadn't known April was such a natural with elders. Especially elders like his father. But she was. His dad was smiling, looking relaxed.

"Mr. Wilkins, these are my children, Eli and Evelyn. Eli, Evelyn, say hi to, uh, Mr. Wilkins. Mr. Frank's father."

"Hi," they chorused, studying Frank's father.

"Hi there, kiddos," he said, leaning forward and holding out a hand to each twin.

After a second's pause, they each took one of his hands and shook it. "Pleased to meet you," Evelyn said.

Frank waited for awkward questions. These kids probably hadn't seen someone like his dad before, someone whose clothes were frayed and none too clean, someone who wore his years of hard living right there in the lines of his face.

But to his surprise, they didn't look fazed by his dad. "Would you like a cookie?" Evelyn asked, pushing the plate of warm cookies toward him.

"We have milk, too," Eli offered.

April smiled and put one hand on Eli's shoulder, the other on Evelyn's. "Please, help yourself," she said, nodding at the cookies. "We have adult beverages, too."

"Hot diggity!" His dad pumped his fist in the air. "I'll take an adult beverage. What you got?"

April dipped her chin like she was unsure how to answer.

Frank went to stand beside April. "Dad. I think April means coffee and tea." He'd never seen alcohol around, didn't think she drank. And for everyone's sake, it would be better if his father didn't.

The man's face fell, but he glanced at the kids and didn't say anything negative. Good. Frank's brothers had told him their father was getting a better filter around kids. "Coffee would be good," he said finally.

"I like your vest." Evelyn had come around the table. She stood about three feet away from his dad, obviously intrigued, but cautious. "Do you ride a motorcycle?"

"As a matter of fact, I do, little lady." His father's eyes crinkled. "Who knows, maybe I'll give you kids a ride one day."

"Dad—"

Frank's father held up a hand. "I know, I know. Motorcycles are dangerous." He smiled down at Evelyn. "Too cold for a ride anyway. I drove over."

"We made a snowman," Eli said from Frank's dad's other side.

"Did you now." Frank's dad looked from Eli to Frank and back again. "Frankie liked to make snowmen, too, when he was a little boy."

"He helped us today!" Evelyn sounded amazed.

"Is that right?" His dad fumbled in his

pocket. "Here, kids, tell you what. If you go watch TV in the other room, I'll give you five dollars."

Eli's eyes went round. "Okay!"

"Five dollars for both of us or to share?" Evelyn put a hand on her hip, looking like a sassy TV teenager.

"Evelyn!" April scolded. "We don't take money from our guests. Go on with Eli." She turned back to the sink.

Frank's father winked at Evelyn and held out a crumpled five-dollar bill. "To share," he stage-whispered.

"Sorry," Frank said to April, keeping his voice low.

She shrugged. "Not a problem."

He loved that about her. She was so relaxed, easy to be with.

His father had walked toward the living room with the twins. Now he came back into the kitchen alone. "The rumor's true," he said. "There's no question those kids are yours. I'm sorry I doubted."

The world stood still.

They were a tableau of three, him staring at his dad, April frozen beside him. His dad stopping still, looking from one to the other.

Around the outer edges of the tableau, everything spun wildly, plates in the air he couldn't begin to keep track of, let alone catch.

His father had just said the twins were Frank's.

April wasn't denying it.

Was she just being polite about an old man's delusions? He turned to her. "That's not right, is it?"

She looked directly into his eyes then, put a hand on his upper arm and nodded. "Your dad's right. The twins are your children."

The mental plates that had been circling in the air seemed to pause, and then they crashed to the ground.

The twins are your children.

The twins are my children.

Eli, with his worried eyes. Take-charge

Evelyn, with enough natural leadership ability to run an army.

Heat suffused his face and neck. His throat tightened and his fists clenched.

"Uh-oh, was this a surprise?" His dad snagged another cookie, went for his coat and shrugged into it. "Sorry, gotta go."

April just stood there, a statue with wide, nervous eyes.

"Wait." Frank caught his father by the sleeve of his coat. "You told me she cheated."

His father's forehead crunched as he concentrated. "She may have," he said, "but maybe she didn't. I had no way of knowing."

"Then why…" Frank trailed off. Why had his father ruined years of Frank's life, to say nothing of what it may have done to April and the kids?

His kids.

"I was mad at her dad. He was a real s—"

April spoke for the first time. "You told

Frank I cheated on him? Because you were mad at my dad?"

"Gotta go." Frank's father pulled away from him.

"Please do." April put her hands to her cheeks, which were flushed red.

Frank walked his father outside, his head spinning. The cold wind felt good.

He had so many things to say to his dad. So many things he wanted to *do* to the man, starting with a punch to the jaw.

But at the moment, his father wasn't the priority. "You okay to drive home?" he asked.

"Fine. Sorry 'bout that." His dad started the car in a hurry and backed out, then the tires squealed in his haste to get away.

Frank's shoulders knotted as he glared after the man. His dad had never vied for Father of the Year, but this was a new pinnacle of bad parenting.

Not even parenting. Just being a bad human being, ruining lives because of your own feud.

And speaking of bad people… He turned and marched back into the house.

April stood, her back against the counter.

He went to stand directly in front of her. More than an arm's length. He wasn't trying to scare her. "The twins are mine?" He had to verify that, one more time. Maybe this had all been a dream.

"Yes," she said. "The twins are yours."

"How do you know for sure?"

Her cheeks flushed. "You were the only possibility."

"That's hard to believe." He'd had years of thinking of her as a cheater. Years of remembering her talking to other guys. And since she'd returned to town with two kids, he'd spent a few bad hours going through acquaintances they'd had when they'd dated: Was that one the father? This one?

She lifted her chin. "Is it harder to believe I'm telling the truth than that your dad was?"

He shelved her question to consider later. Right now, he had a fight to pick. "I'll confirm it with a DNA test, so the truth's going to come out."

"It…it just did." Her voice sounded breathless, like she'd been working out.

"Any particular reason you never told me?" He kept his voice quiet. Crossed his arms over his chest.

"There were a couple of reasons," she said.

Fury rushed over him. "What reason could there be?" he shouted.

She shook her head, patted the air in a "quiet down" gesture. She craned around him toward the door. Sounds of a TV show came from the other room.

"I'll talk to you if you'll refrain from yelling and upsetting the kids."

My kids. He swallowed hard, nodded. His head felt like it was about to explode.

"Number one," she said, speaking rapidly in a low voice. "My dad would have killed you. Literally. He'd have figured it out. He knew we were seeing each other. In fact…" She looked away, blinking rapidly.

"What?" He wasn't going to be placated by her tears.

"When he found out I was pregnant, he wanted to know who had done it, and he wouldn't let up. I had to tell him I didn't know, that there were a few possibilities."

"So let me get this straight." Frank studied her face, torn between anger and confusion and wonder. "You spread the word that you were sleeping around to protect me? That's a little hard to believe."

"I didn't spread the word. I told my dad." She clutched the counter like she needed it for support. "Believe what you want."

"You said there were reasons. And sit down." He pulled out a kitchen chair for her and went to the opposite side of the table to face her. Couldn't have her collapsing before she revealed the whole sordid truth.

She flopped into the chair. "In spite of my dad's potential for violence, I came to your parents' house to try and talk to you."

"I never heard about that," he said, doubting the truth of it.

"You were gone. Your dad and mom wouldn't tell me where. Said you wanted nothing to do with me."

"You believed them?"

"Yes, I did, Frank. Because I never heard one more word from you after I found out I was expecting. You left town, weeks before you had to be back on your base, with no forwarding address." She paused. "I guess I could have found out the address of your base and hunted you down, but I was in pretty bad shape mentally."

For the first time, he imagined what all that would feel like to a pregnant eighteen-year-old. Sympathy and shame tried to rise in his heart, but he shoved them away. He still had questions.

"Your dad passed away last year," he said. "So excuse number one is no longer relevant. And you met me again five, six weeks ago. You knew where to find me after that. In fact, you were living with me. That takes out excuse number two."

"The book had to take priority," she said. For the first time, she sounded unsure.

He pounced on that. "The book took priority over your, supposedly my, kids?" The meaning of it all was washing over him. All the times they'd shared a meal or a movie, this very day when they'd hiked and built a snowman, they'd been a family.

She was the only one who'd known the secret. Had she reveled in that?

Had she been the only one? Or had everyone known but him? Dad had mentioned rumors. "Do the twins know?"

"Of course not!" She shook her head rapidly.

More rage surged inside and erupted. "You let me abandon them!" Making him a worse father than his own sorry excuse for one. "You kept me out of their lives."

A small hand tugging at his sleeve pulled him back together, instantly. He looked down.

"You were shouting," Evelyn said. "Eli is scared."

Eli walked in to stand beside his sister.

"Come here, kids." April perched on the edge of her chair and pulled them into her arms. After a hug, she let them go and faced them. "Grown-ups have arguments sometimes," she said. "Mr. Frank and I are having an argument, but it's for the adults to work out, not you."

He couldn't imagine how she kept her voice so calm.

But then, she was used to comforting them. Because she'd gotten to raise them.

Evelyn pushed a lock of hair behind her ear and looked at him, eyebrows drawing together. Her expression was a mix of scared kid and avenging superhero.

Just that look made him smile, and a wave of tenderness washed over him. He looked into her eyes and then into Eli's. "I'm sorry I scared you. I won't yell anymore."

"Okay," Evelyn said. "Can we play with Dozer?"

"Sure," he said distractedly. Clearly, the little girl wanted to stay close by, in case any loud arguments broke out again.

He felt like yelling at April some more, but he couldn't scare the children.

He needed to be by himself and think. Needed it badly. But he *lived* here with this beautiful, maddening trio. With these kids, whose childhood he had missed.

"You know what," he said to April. "I need to do a couple of things out of the house."

"Okay," she said. He couldn't tell if that was relief or just exhaustion in her voice. She'd been keeping that secret a long time. "But we should talk soon."

"We should have talked a while back, like six years ago."

"That wasn't an option for me, as I've explained." Her voice was as even as his. More even.

The kids played with Dozer in a cozy

corner of the kitchen. April looked at him expectantly with those big blue-green eyes. "We can work this out, Frank."

Could they? He doubted it. "Later. I'm going out."

"What about Dozer?"

"He can stay. I gotta go." Feeling somehow cowardly, he strode out of the house without a coat and got into his truck with the thought of driving as fast and as far away as possible.

Chapter Thirteen

As she sat on a small chair in the Sunday school classroom, checking kids out to their parents at the end of services, April was wearily proud of herself. She'd held it together, just like she'd held it together for most of a difficult week.

Six days ago, Frank had found out the truth about the children and stalked out of the house with more unfinished business than could have been hauled in his truck. She'd hidden in the bathroom and let herself freak out for just a few minutes. Then she'd pulled herself together, made a plan and sent him two texts:

Not telling kids until we've talked. Best for them. Please respect my decision.

And

I'll integrate what we learned on the trip and send to you section by section. You can revise, put it together and submit. Agent can extend deadline to Monday if necessary. Will work as fast as possible.

Most of the kids were heading out with their parents, but a few remained and the twins were playing with them. Including Bentley the Bully, to April's surprise. He and Eli were putting together a long toy train, assisted by Jodi's son JJ.

Darci Mae walked in, her hair perfect, wearing an emerald green designer dress. She scanned the room and found the boys. "You're letting them build something now?"

April was too spent to get defensive. "Figured I'd rather clean up a mess than mediate a fight. They're getting along, so why mess with success?"

Darci Mae tilted her head to one side. "Point taken." She walked over to her son. "Bentley, come on."

"No!" The boy hunched away from Darci Mae and kept putting together train cars.

"Eli," Evelyn said, "time to clean up."

Eli frowned, considering. "Only if *he* helps."

Evelyn went over to Bentley and squatted down beside him. "You hafta help clean up now," she said.

"No."

Evelyn stood and put her hands on her hips. "It's a *rule*!" She pointed at the clock. "It's time to clean up!"

Darci Mae blinked. "Can she tell time already?"

April laughed. "No. She's just seen me point at the clock a lot."

Eli started taking train cars apart and tossing them into a plastic bin. "Score!"

he said each time a toy hit the bin. JJ grabbed one of the train cars and started doing the same.

Bentley watched for a minute, and then joined in.

"It's a noisy way of getting everything cleaned up," April commented to Darci Mae, "but I'll take the help."

"Yeah." Darci Mae studied her. "You look tired."

"But still gorgeous." Jodi, the main teacher in the Sunday school class this week, came over and joined them, giving April a curious glance.

"Thanks. I'm going to clean up." She excused herself and went to fold a heap of dress-up clothes as the other two women chatted.

She had to think.

But she was in no shape to do it.

Was it viable to stay in Holiday Point? That was the question that kept rolling around in her mind. It was decision time, and she had no idea of the right course.

She'd been working twenty-hour days to finish the book. As promised, she'd sent sections to Frank by email. He'd responded tersely, "Received," and a couple of times, had sent clarification questions. That had been their only contact.

April had taken breaks from her work only to feed the kids. She'd let them watch way too much TV.

It had been the only way to get through after the shock of having the truth about the twins blurted out to Frank. And then, to get through the fact that he'd left. He hadn't come back except when she was out of the house. She could tell because of tire tracks and footprints in the snow, and because a few folders and files were gone from their shared office.

On Friday morning, she'd sent the rest of the book to him. He'd either edit it that day or over the weekend, and then send it off to their agent.

And just like that, her work on the book and with him was done.

She should have collapsed in happy relief, but instead, she'd continued on a high wire of anxiety, trying to find balance and figure out answers to all the questions she had.

When would it be right to tell the kids? How would Frank even act with them? How would he be as a father?

Had he continued to be angry? Where was he, anyway?

Along with the questions, guilt had churned inside her. When you got down to it, she'd concealed the truth from someone extremely important in the kids' lives. She'd kept their father from them, and them from their father.

She folded the last sparkly headdress and put the stack into the dress-up box. Darci Mae and Bentley were just leaving, and April was shocked to see Bentley hug Eli. At least she'd done something right, if her son could be that sweet to a kid he'd been at odds with just a few weeks ago.

Well, she and Frank had done something right. She couldn't deny that he'd helped Eli fit into his new school.

And there it was: she was back to thinking about Frank. The same swirling thoughts that had kept her awake for the past two nights, even after the manuscript was turned in.

Jodi marched over. "How *are* you?"

"What do you mean? Why are you asking?" April was stalling.

"I mean, you look upset. And tired, like Darci Mae was kind enough to point out. And I know that Frank moved out, because he's staying with us."

April blew out a breath. One question answered.

She looked at Jodi's sympathetic face, and a great desire for a friend washed over her. Jodi had been nothing but sweet to her, and as far as April knew, she hadn't shared any secrets that she'd learned about April. She wasn't a gossip.

Why not talk with her openly?

She was about the only person April would consider telling. "Frank found out about the twins," she said.

Jodi's eyes widened and her forehead creased. "Oh, no. I'm guessing he didn't take it well."

April shrugged. "He didn't *say* anything bad, but I haven't spoken to him since he found out. Until just a minute ago, I didn't know where he was."

"Oh, honey." Jodi hugged her, holding on for an extra comforting few seconds. "How are *you* doing?"

April blinked a few times and looked over toward the twins and JJ. They were getting more blocks out of another bin, scattering them over an area of floor Jodi had already vacuumed. Oh, well. "I'm hanging in there," she said, her voice only slightly shaky.

"Well, Frank's a mess," Jodi said. "But I figured it was finishing the book that was making him look all haggard. Now I know differently."

"He's busy with that, too. I'm done with my part, and he should be done with his by tomorrow."

Jodi frowned. "So, what does that mean for you and the kids?"

"That's exactly what I'm trying to figure out." She turned to the twins. "Evelyn. Eli. Put the blocks away. We need to get going."

Jodi gripped her hand. "I'm here for you. If you need a girls' night, a listening ear, babysitting…whatever. You don't have to go it alone."

April's throat tightened, so that she could barely choke out, "Thank you."

"And come to our Super Bowl party tonight." She told April the details before April could protest that she wasn't in a party mood. "Promise you'll think about it, at least."

"I'll think about it."

The last couple of kids were checked out, and Jodi headed out, too, JJ running beside her. Eli and Evelyn did a quick job of cleaning up blocks and ran off to follow them after promising to wait at the back of the church, not to go out into the parking lot.

April walked slowly behind them as she pondered the question Jodi had asked. What did finishing the book mean for her or the kids?

It was what had been rolling around in her head for the past forty-eight hours. As well as before that.

Was Holiday Point the place for them? Yes, she had an interview for a teacher's aide job next week, and a couple of leads on rentals in town. But could they live here, at odds with Frank?

Across the sanctuary, she saw Frank, talking to Cam. Her heart stuttered, then settled into a rapid pounding.

His eyes were bloodshot, his beard stubble made him look either rugged or derelict depending on your point of view, and every year he'd lived was etched onto his face. For the first time, she noticed a resemblance to his father.

She'd done that to him?

Her chest ached as if she'd run a marathon and didn't know whether she'd won or lost. Seeing Frank shouldn't make her this emotional. They'd worked together for almost six weeks without drama.

She should at least try to regain that professionalism and use it to detach. But it was wretchedly difficult to detach from the father of your children. Especially if he was your first love, and you'd never really loved anyone else, and you felt like an adoring puppy every time you saw him.

The pastor patted her arm. "Just checking in," he said. "Is everything okay?"

At that point April realized she'd been standing in the center aisle of the church while most everyone departed the building. Given that two people had already told her she looked bad, and now she was close to tears…yeah. No wonder the pastor had wanted to check in.

"Can I pray for you or with you?" he asked.

"I guess figuring out when someone's in trouble goes with the job description," she said, making him smile. "I'd appreciate it a lot if you'd pray with me."

Frank was speaking with Cam, waiting for Jodi and the kids so they could head back to Cam's house.

But Jodi marched over alone. She stood in front of Frank, hands on hips. "You found out," she said. "About the twins."

"Yeah," he was surprised into saying. When Cam didn't question Jodi, Frank looked at him. "You're not surprised?"

Cam shrugged. "Guessed."

"And you didn't tell me?"

"Never mind that." Jodi glared at Frank. "You haven't spoken to her since you found out? She's a wreck."

Frank held up his hands, wanting to block the attack. "She didn't tell me. She worked with me for nearly six weeks, lived in the same house with me, without revealing the tiny little fact that the twins were my children."

"Can you even imagine what the past six years have been like for her?" Jodi asked. "Pregnant and then raising twins alone, with the dad AWOL?"

"I didn't—"

"Don't get defensive, just put yourself in her shoes for a minute. She's had a hard path."

Reluctantly, because they were in church and he ought to be nice, he let Jodi's words create an image in his mind: April, pregnant, leaving town who knew how, starting a life in a strange city, alone.

"But then why didn't she tell me, once she saw me?"

Jodi and Cam glanced at each other.

"Are you that far away from being poor?" Cam asked. "She quit her job and moved her kids on the strength of the job she had with you. Obviously, telling you would have jeopardized that. Look how you reacted when you did find out. You bolted."

"And she's got only herself to depend on, financially," Jodi said. "Since there was no father in the picture to offer child support."

Child support. Of course, she could have and should have demanded it. He scrubbed a hand over his chin. He would put together a plan to pay it back to her. That was only right.

He looked up and there she was, talking to the pastor, smiling through tears it looked like, and the man had a hand on her shoulder, speaking earnestly.

The guy wanted her, obviously. Possessiveness surged. "Why's the pastor talking to her so much? He doesn't even know her. Does he?"

Cam raised an eyebrow, looking askance at Frank. "He's the pastor. His job is to talk to people."

"Come on," Jodi said, taking Frank's arm. "You'll see them later."

"See who?"

"She and the twins are coming to the Super Bowl party tonight, at least I think so, and I expect you to act decent around them," she said.

"Speaking of, you two need to tell the kids," Cam added. "Doesn't have to be today, but soon."

Frank watched as the twins ran to April from the back of the church, one hugging each of her legs. She smiled and put a hand on each red-gold head. The pastor knelt in front of them and spoke to the kids, smiling at them, obviously asking questions. They responded with smiles and animation.

Frank watched, and reminded himself that this was the guy's job, and felt jealous anyway. Possessive of the kids, just like he was possessive of April.

Christians were instructed to care for the fatherless. That was what the Bible said.

Well, his kids weren't fatherless. Not anymore.

And the sooner they found out and started benefiting from having him as a father, the better. Maybe even today.

Chapter Fourteen

When April and the twins arrived at the party, it was a swarm of people already. Probably because they were running late. April had been the one procrastinating, while the twins had been eager to get going.

To see their cousins, although they still thought of the other kids as just friends. Wonderful new friends. Their adoration of Frank's brothers' kids was so sweet.

Already comfortable at Cam and Jodi's house, Eli and Evelyn rushed inside, greeting Hector and JJ with special enthusiasm. April followed, and most everyone stood to greet them, hugging April like she was one of their own.

Everyone except Frank. He stood off to the side, looking wary.

Well, he *should* be wary, because she felt ready to punch him in the nose. He'd abandoned her again. This time, he'd abandoned her *and* the twins.

As a result of her talk with the pastor and a lot of thinking and praying, she'd figured out what today was all about.

Tell the truth and say goodbye.

One thing she hated about the whole mess was deceiving the other women, Frank's brothers' wives. They'd been nothing but kind to her, not knowing that the twins were their kids' cousins.

If there was a chance to get the women alone, she'd talk to them about it. Knowing them, they might even have good advice for her as well.

She could use some advice, because now, watching Frank look at the twins with naked hunger in his eyes, she felt ready to fall apart.

An arm came around her. "You doing okay?" Jodi asked.

As Frank started to walk across the room toward her, she swallowed the huge lump in her throat. "I'm okay," she rasped.

Jodi stepped away as Frank reached her. Somehow everyone was slipping away. Reflexively she reached for the kids, but even Eli was across the room with Olivia's son, Freddie, and his dog.

Frank stopped in front of her, a good arm's length away. He ran a hand through his already-messy hair. "I delivered the book manuscript. Thank you for all your work on it."

"You're welcome." If he could play it cool, so could she.

But her heart wasn't remotely cool. It was reaching out for him with an impossible longing. Why, oh, why did she still have feelings for him, this man who had abandoned her not once but twice?

She nodded toward the big plate of brownies she was holding. "I'd better take this to the kitchen. Good to see you." She blinked and swallowed hard as she turned away and started toward the kitchen.

Evelyn was playing some kind of game with foam balls, laughing and shouting with the other kids. She tossed a ball to Eli, and he caught it and joined in.

Their cousins.

They loved this so much, loved being a part of things.

She glanced back at Frank to see him looking at her, eyes burning.

She tore her gaze away and marched into the kitchen, where most of the women had gathered. Kelly, Alec's wife, was talking to Jodi about pregnancy while Olivia and another woman who had to be her sister chopped veggies for a relish plate.

Fisk, the only man in the room, was stirring something in a big mixing bowl while his wife, Lauren, leaned back against the counter beside him, smiling up at him.

April was so fond of Jodi and Olivia, and she was getting to know and like Frank's other brothers and their wives as well. Keeping this from them was just another bad part of the whole mess.

She made a snap decision. She was done with it.

She put down her brownies and rushed back out to where Frank now stood beside Cam, watching a football replay. She tapped his arm and beckoned him away. "I'm going to tell the women," she said quietly. "I wanted you to know."

He frowned and shook his head. "I don't think that's wise. Won't word spread to their kids? And then to the twins?"

She lifted her hands, palms up. "I don't know. I don't think so."

"Then I'll tell my brothers, I guess. But I want us to tell the twins. As soon as possible."

She studied his face. "Have you thought about what that will mean? You can't hurt them. I won't allow it."

One of the kids misfired a foam ball, and it shot toward them. Frank reached out, caught it and tossed it back without looking away from April. "Hurting them is the last thing I want," he said.

"If you let them know, though, there will be expectations. A lot of them. On their part."

"I want to be their father," he said simply.

His softly spoken words made April's stomach turn over. He wanted to be their father.

She knew him well enough to understand that if he made that commitment, he'd keep it. "Let's talk later," she said, "about how to tell them."

She straightened her shoulders and went back into the kitchen. She whispered to Jodi, who nodded and then waved her arm. "Hey, everyone. Attention. This kitchen is officially women-only for the next hour. The men's job is to keep the kids out. Spread the word," she said to Fisk.

He wiped his hands, nodding, and gave his wife a peck on the cheek. After he left, Jodi looked around the room. "Listen up, everyone. April wants to talk to us. Frank's brothers' wives."

Olivia held up her knife. "I'll leave, if one of you wants to finish cutting up veggies," she said.

"It's okay, Olivia. You can stay. You feel like family."

Olivia's sister headed for the door. "I'll be out there with the guys," she said. "I already have too much drama in my life."

Olivia looked after her worriedly. "She really does," she murmured. "But this isn't about my sister. This is about April."

They all gathered around the big kitchen table.

Jodi put out an old-fashioned teapot and passed around cups. "And I think we have first dibs on April's brownies," she said. "Everything's easier with chocolate."

As she put the brownies and a small stack of plates on the table, April jumped in. "I have something to tell you guys, but it's got to be a cone of silence. Especially, the kids can't know."

"You can trust us," Kelly said, and the others chimed in, nodding, looking concerned.

April believed them. "It's about the kids. My kids." She cleared her throat and blurted it out. "They're also Frank's."

"Frank's the *father*?" Olivia squeaked.

"He never said anything," Kelly said. "How did he keep that to himself?"

"Do they know?" someone else said, but April couldn't even keep track of who.

Jodi put two fingers to her mouth and whistled. "Hey! Let the woman tell the story."

April's heart pounded, but the tension that usually resided around her neck and shoulders eased a little as she took in the curious, but essentially friendly, faces around her. "Not that great of a story," she said. "When Frank and I dated, the summer I was eighteen, I got pregnant. Apparently, about the same time, Frank's father told him I was cheating on him."

Various expressions of dismay. She held up a hand. "Before you ask…it wasn't true. There was no one else." Not ever, physically or emotionally or spiritually. For better or worse, it had always been Frank. "From what I've been able to figure out, Frank heard that, believed it and left town. And that's what he thought until, well, about a week ago."

Jaws dropped. "All that time?" Olivia asked. "How?"

"Secrets are toxic," Kelly said, frowning, her expression severe.

"They are," April said, "but my father was *really* toxic. I'm pretty sure he would have killed Frank if he'd found out. And I'm not speaking metaphorically."

"I heard there was a grudge between your dad and Mr. Wilkins," Lauren said. "Fisk and I talked about it. He knows."

"If you didn't know April's dad," Jodi

said, looking around, "he was a cop, and super strict."

"Angry," Kelly said, nodding. "So I heard. And he was one of those cops who walked around armed all the time, even off duty, I'm assuming?"

"All the time." April swallowed hard, thinking of the small arsenal she'd found when an aunt had invited her to help clear out the house after her father had died. It had hurt terribly that she hadn't heard about his death until a week after the funeral. Since then, she'd worked hard to overcome her own bitterness, knowing it would hurt no one but herself. "He wasn't a bad man as long as I toed the line. He was actually fun before my mom passed away."

Olivia put an arm around her. "You've had a hard row to hoe," she said.

"Kinda." April couldn't embrace the sympathy. She was already too much on the edge, emotionally. These women's kindness made her want to burst into tears, but she was afraid she'd never stop crying.

And of course, she had to keep it together, because she was a mom.

"Anyway," she said, wanting to get the whole story out, "our dads were lifelong enemies. When I showed up pregnant it was bad enough, but I wouldn't reveal the babies' father to my dad. The whole thing led to some pretty awful fights, and in the end, he disowned me. Kicked me out."

"Oh, wow. And then he died." Lauren leaned over and gave April a side hug. "That must have been hard to deal with."

"How did Frank find out?" Kelly asked. "Did you tell him?"

"I wish I had," she said, sighing. "I meant to, I just… I figured it would be rough, and I wanted us to finish his book first. But his dad came over, and when he saw the twins, he noticed similarities between Frank and Eli and made the connection. It came out that he'd lied about my cheating." She had to smile a little, remembering the expression on Mr. Wilkins's face. "When he realized what he'd done, that Frank didn't know the twins were his, he hightailed it out of there. It was almost funny."

Olivia blew out a breath. "Almost, but not. So, have you talked much to Frank about it?"

She shook her head. "He kinda...bailed on me. Took off after he heard. We completed the book by email, but we haven't talked, except for a couple of minutes today."

Amidst indignant murmurs, Lauren spoke up. "The kids don't know?"

"No. And I don't know how to tell them. He wants to, though. He said that today." She swallowed hard. "I'm so confused."

Kelly leaned forward. "Suggestion. I know a family counselor over in Uniontown. She helped us when we had to tell Zinnia that there were parts of her story she didn't know." She started searching through her phone. "I'll send you her contact information."

"That's a good idea." April heaved out a

breath, relieved. Of course. A professional counselor would know how to approach the matter in the way that worked best for young kids.

"Nobody here has had a perfect life," Jodi said. "And we all know how hard it is to be a mom. We'll help in any way we can."

The other women nodded in agreement.

April looked around the circle of friendly, concerned faces. "Thanks for not judging me or putting me down. I know it's a lot."

The murmured responses were kind, and they took turns hugging her.

"That must have been so hard," Olivia said. "I think you're really brave."

"We want you to be a part of the family," Jodi said, her voice earnest. "You and the kids. You belong here in Holiday Point, with the whole family."

April sipped her tea, trying to loosen the lump in her throat. It just felt so good, deep in her soul, to belong. "I want that, too," she managed to say. "Believe me. So much. But…it really hurts to see Frank."

"Why?" Olivia looked puzzled. "Now that the secret's out, can't you work it out? I'd think you would be so motivated."

April splayed her hands and shook her head. "I don't think so. Look how Frank responded to the news. He abandoned me for the second time. Ran away." And this time, he'd abandoned his kids, too.

Although that wasn't fair. He'd just told her he wanted to be their father.

Which was good and admirable, but where did it leave April? How was she supposed to turn into a distantly friendly co-parent with the man who had her heart?

She was supposed to talk to him after the party, to decide what to do about telling the kids. She'd share the information Kelly had offered, about the family counselor. But the thought of seeing him…of sitting and talking civilly to this wonderful man who seemed always to be running away from her...she couldn't even imagine how that was going to work.

Frank spent most of the party brooding about the upcoming conversation with April. Brooding because he *did* want to talk about being the twins' father. That was an identity that had risen up and wrapped instantly around his heart, changing him forever.

But fatherhood wasn't the only change pushing at him. Every time he'd turned around in the past week, her image had flashed across his mind. April throwing snowballs with the twins, her hair flowing wildly. April bent over his shoulder, looking at something on his computer screen, smelling like flowers.

April looking miserable as she'd told him the story of what had happened.

The outlines, at least. He had many, many questions.

What he wanted, along with answers and along with taking part in the twins'

330 The Veteran's Valentine Helper

futures, was to make a family with her. To build a life with her, or try to. Maybe it wouldn't work, but the fact that they both still had feelings after six years apart meant something. He wanted to find out what.

A child's scream pierced his thoughts. It sounded like Eli, and Frank was instantly on his feet and running.

Sure enough, in the basement playroom, Eli wailed and pointed at Evelyn. And Evelyn was...yeah. Throwing up. Not for the first time, it looked like. He rushed over and knelt beside her.

"She said she felt sick, and then she barfed!" Hector told him.

"A lot!" his little brother, JJ, said with what sounded like admiration.

"Okay. Okay, honey." He put an arm around her shoulders, tentatively. "You'll feel better pretty soon."

"Direct quote from Mom," Frank's brother Cam said. He disappeared into the laundry room for a moment, then returned with a wet washcloth and a couple of hand towels. "Clean her up when she's ready, and we'll put her on the couch. JJ, get a roll of paper towels."

Frank wiped Evelyn's teary face, carried her away from the mess she'd made and tucked her wispy hair behind her ears. She smelled terrible, of course.

To his own shock, Frank didn't mind.

Instead, his heart just about overflowed with joy, because he was taking care of *his daughter*. He ran the cloth over her hands and then, when he realized more cleanup was needed, he took her to the bathroom to better wash her hands and get her a paper cup of water. "Just sip a little, honey," he said. "Get the taste out of your mouth. That's it."

As they emerged from the bathroom, he marveled. He kind of felt like a father.

Cam was using paper towels and some kind of spray to clean up the floor.

"Sorry, man," Frank said as he carried Evelyn by.

Cam looked up, and the expression in his younger brother's eyes was steady and knowing.

Because of course, it had come out after church today. Cam knew the twins were his. Jodi, too.

No time for a conversation, though. Eli escaped from the grip of his cousin Zinnia, who'd apparently been comforting him. He ran alongside Frank, jumping up. "Okay, Evie?" he asked, grabbing on to his sister's foot. "Yuck, your foot's wet."

"You got throw-up on you!" JJ pointed, then leaned closer to see.

"Come on, we'll get you cleaned up, too," Frank said, reaching down and guiding Eli into the bathroom with a hand on the back of his neck.

Helping Eli wash his hands, helping Evelyn change into a clean shirt Cam handed in to him while the cousins crowded around the door looking on, Frank felt almost proud. Not of his skill at child care—he was pretty clumsy with it—but of his brothers and their kids. A Wilkins, proud of his family! But he could see how much this gaggle of cousins and uncles and aunts could offer kids like Eli and Evelyn, who had few other relatives.

His side of the family could be good for the twins. Could add something to their lives. And no, he wasn't happy to have missed out on sharing them with his brothers' families all these years, but look what could lie ahead.

He and April just had to come to terms with each other. Hammer something out. Make it work for Eli and Evelyn's sake.

There was no time for working anything out that night. As soon as April came in, having finally been told that Evelyn was sick, a more professional air came over things. She felt the twins' foreheads, and consulted with Jodi, and decided they should leave right away, hopefully without having infecting any of the other kids.

"No telling who infected who," Jodi said, shrugging. "I'm sure most of them will

334 *The Veteran's Valentine Helper*

catch it, or something else. It's that time of year."

Frank remembered that from childhood, hadn't thought of it in years: how as soon as one of his four brothers got sick, the rest of them would quickly follow suit.

He'd never before considered what that was like for his parents, though, or more realistically, for his mom.

Frank didn't even consider staying behind. They made it home without another vomiting episode, but both twins had a turn at it later that night. Their temperatures were elevated, but not into a scary range according to April.

It was all scary to Frank. And yet in some ways it all felt so normal.

He'd been jealous of his brothers' families, and here it looked like he'd acquired one of his own.

What format that family would take was a question that hummed along the back of his consciousness as he ran out for fever medicine and wiped faces and read stories. For the first time, he followed April into the twins' little bedroom and helped Eli put on superhero pajamas while April helped Evelyn. He read them a few more stories, and finally, both kids slept.

He pulled a cover up over Eli and took a little plastic doll out of Evelyn's grip. "Good night," he tried to say. But his throat had closed up.

He looked at them for a moment longer, trying to savor and make sense of this expanding feeling in his chest. He'd do anything, absolutely anything, for these kids. Just like that, he'd grown a father's heart.

He turned, and April stood in the doorway, watching him. She gave him a funny half smile. Then she headed downstairs, with Frank following, and flung herself into an overstuffed chair. "Man, I'm tired."

She *looked* tired. "Get some sleep while you can," he said. "We don't have to talk about anything deep tonight."

"No, we should," she protested. "I heard

about this counselor who helps families with stuff like this." She yawned hugely.

"Come on." He stood above her and held out his hands to pull her up. "Go sleep in your own comfortable bed. Plenty of time to talk tomorrow."

He had a different perspective on the conversation, now that he'd started fathering for real.

Chapter Fifteen

On Wednesday morning, April watched Evelyn and Eli eat their breakfast of eggs and toast. They'd eaten a little yesterday, but this was the first time they'd shown enthusiasm for food.

"Is there more?" Evelyn asked. Eli held out his plate, too.

Frank brought their plates to the stove for a refill and popped two more pieces of toast into the toaster. "Remember, though," he said to the kids, "you've been sick. Eat slowly."

"We're all better," Eli said, flashing a smile at Frank.

Thank heavens. She'd been praying that they would recover enough to go to school on Valentine's Day. They really, really wanted to go, and April *had* to go, since she was responsible for organizing and directing the party, along with Jodi.

As Frank carried the plates of eggs over, then came back to butter toast, April's heart twisted and turned like a hippie-style lava lamp.

Since Sunday night, Frank had gotten a crash course in parenting. Taking care of two sick six-year-olds was not for the weak. But he'd insisted on helping, had carried spit pans and taken temperatures and changed sheets. Once that phase was over, he'd helped entertain the twins during their enforced twenty-four-hour fever-free period that had to precede them returning to school.

He'd gone back to his own half of the house at night, but the rest of the time, he'd been right there with her, co-parenting. When she'd thanked him, he'd shrugged.

"I'm their father," he'd said in a quiet voice only she could hear. "It's my responsibility just as much as yours. More, because I'm making up for all the times I didn't take care of them."

She'd searched his face for anger, but she hadn't found it. Maybe he was just too exhausted to remain furious at her that she hadn't told him about the twins. Neither of them had gotten much sleep.

April was too tired to fight with him about abandoning her twice, that was for sure. She was thankful that he wasn't abandoning her now. He'd even insisted she take a nap each afternoon, or some time for herself to read or take a walk, while he cared for the kids solo.

He was getting to know them, learning how to be a father.

"I'm ready for school!" Evelyn announced, pushing aside her plate full of seconds.

"Me, too," Eli said, following suit.

April's phone rang, and she took the call

from Jodi. "Are you ready for today?" she asked her friend. Because Jodi really was that. She'd checked in on April and the twins each day, and had brought over a pot of homemade chicken noodle soup that had made all of them feel loved.

"I'm *not* ready," Jodi said, her voice husky. "I'm sick. I can't do the party with you. Hang on." She must have covered the phone, because the sound of her racking cough was muffled.

"Oh, no!" April was dismayed, but also concerned. "I hope the kids didn't give you whatever they had. How can I help?"

"I'm fine, Cam took today off. He's a good nurse." Jodi coughed again. "But I'm really sorry I can't be there. Will you manage okay?"

"Of course," April said firmly, though her heart sank at the thought of running a party for twenty first-graders by herself.

"Maybe one of the other moms can help," Jodi croaked out. "Or Frank."

"We'll figure it out. Go lie down, and

call me if you think of something I can pick up for you."

As she ended the call, Frank started clearing breakfast dishes. "Go brush your teeth," he said to the twins.

They looked over at April. After a nod from her, they ran toward the bathroom.

She sat down at the table and chugged half her cup of cold coffee. "What am I going to do? This party is practically my audition for Holiday Point motherhood, and it's already falling apart."

Frank tipped his head to one side. "Jodi's sick?"

"Yep. And she was supposed to help me with the party today."

"The one the other moms bailed on," he said. He paused, then nodded decisively. "I'll come and help."

"What?" She was shocked at the offer, even though Jodi had suggested Frank as a possible replacement. "You don't have to do that."

He shrugged. "Why should it all be on the mother?"

"Um, because most men don't handle groups of excited young children that well?"

"Maybe you're right," he acknowledged. "Most men take fatherhood for granted. Even my brothers, from time to time. But not me. I'm making up for lost time and I want every moment I can get."

The kids came down the stairs in double time.

"Is it okay with you two," he said, "if I come help at your Valentine's party?"

"Yes! Yay!" Evelyn jumped up and down. Eli went over and leaned against Frank's leg, smiling.

April's stomach twisted.

Even though she was grateful for the help, even though the kids' excitement made her smile, she couldn't help worrying. What if Frank's interest in fatherhood was fleeting? What if he bailed on them again?

* * *

The questions about Frank still bothered April as they were buzzed into the elementary school that afternoon.

He *seemed* fine with coming, and he was carrying a big plastic tub full of juice boxes, water bottles and cookies. April tried not to look at him too much, but the man had serious muscles that looked amazing in his short-sleeved T-shirt. He wasn't even wearing a jacket in this misty, fifty-degree weather.

"You sure about this?" she asked as they headed down the hall toward the twins' classroom.

"Of course. We're done with the book, so I have time. And, well, they're my kids."

"Shh!" She'd just spotted Darci Mae walking ahead of them into the classroom. What was she doing here? She'd quit the party committee.

When they walked into the room, the kids were busy at stations, but there was a lot of excited chatter. Upon seeing the adults arrive with supplies, a couple of kids left their seats and ran toward them.

Olivia blinked the lights on and off. "Children. You need to continue quietly working. Once you've finished your work and the grown-ups have done some setup, we'll have our party."

Immediately, the children focused—or pretended to—on their work.

April and Frank set down their materials. With Olivia's help, they organized a snack table and a craft table.

"Could you grab the other end?" April asked Darci Mae as she tried to move a heavy cabinet at Olivia's suggestion.

"Oh, no, I'm just here to take pictures. I wouldn't want to interfere with your ideas."

Okay, Ms. Passive Aggressive, I get it.

Olivia came over and lifted the opposite end of the cabinet. After they'd moved it, she turned to Darci Mae. "Parents are always welcome in my classroom," she said, "but I prefer that you give me some notice.

And any parent here may be called on to help."

"I didn't dress for that." Darci Mae slid her hands down the hips of her pencil skirt. Then she gave Frank a big smile.

April glanced down at her jeans and sweater. Frumpy, for sure, and she felt a surge of jealousy for Darci Mae's expensive clothes and skillfully applied makeup.

Lord, help my attitude.

Frank had seen her at her worst these past few days, much worse than this, and he'd stuck around. He'd even given her a few intense looks, and she hadn't deserved them based on her grungy outfits and dirty hair.

At least today she'd showered!

She wasn't going to let Darci Mae affect her emotions, nor her plans. Being in Holiday Point was just what she needed for her kids, and she was determined to stay. A check from completing the book had just landed in her account, and she had a lead on a place to live.

"Ready if you are," she said to Frank and Olivia.

"How many children are finished with your work?" Olivia called out.

The clamor of affirmatives was deafening. Frank winced.

Olivia nodded at April, and she moved into her first game, a rowdy round of musical hearts. Next, they played the math-and-letters game, which the kids surprisingly enjoyed, though Darci Mae sneered. The homemade cookies were a hit.

Everything went well, but too quickly. There were twenty minutes left in the school day, and April had a moment of panic. What did you do with twenty sugared-up first-graders for twenty minutes? Left to their own devices, they'd run around yelling and shoving each other. In fact, a few girls were already doing just that.

Frank was kneeling by the bookshelves. He pulled out a story that had exactly nothing to do with Valentine's Day, but it did have a lot of animals in it. April smiled. He'd read the book to Eli and Evelyn several times.

"Okay, kids, come sit up here for a story," he called in his deep voice.

"Carpet squares, with comfortable space in between," Olivia announced, then turned to April. "That keeps them at arm's length."

As soon as the children were settled, Frank started reading in his deep, rumbling voice.

"Never fails," Olivia said to April. "The dad voice keeps them on good behavior. Are you doing okay?"

The kids chortled as Frank made his first series of animal sounds.

"I'm fine," she said. "Just so glad the kids were well enough to come to school today."

"Me, too," Olivia said. "Look how much better Bentley behaves when the twins are with him."

April looked. Indeed, Bentley sat in between the two children. When he reached forward to do something to another child, Evelyn tapped him on the arm and shook her head, and he stopped.

April had to laugh.

Olivia joined in. "Evelyn's amazing when she uses her powers for good."

As the story finished, Bentley pointed at Frank. "Is he your daddy?" he asked Eli, his high-pitched voice carrying across the room.

April's world went still. This was *not* how she wanted the kids to find out. Would the very notion shock them?

"Yeah," Eli said nonchalantly.

Evelyn nodded matter-of-factly.

Darci Mae looked wide-eyed from April to Frank and back again.

Frank stood and walked over to put the book back as Olivia took over the class again to get the kids ready for buses and car pool. While they were occupied, April went over to him. "You didn't tell them, did you?"

"Nope. Did you?"

She shook her head.

"Then how do they know?" he asked her in a whisper.

She shrugged, lifting her hands. "I guess kids know more than you think," she said. "That's what the counselor said when I made the appointment. She said they might already sense or assume it."

"Wild." He looked down for a minute, then looked up at her with an expression so burning that she blushed. "We need to talk," he said quietly. "Soon. Tonight if possible."

"Uh…okay." Her heart was pounding rapidly. *We need to talk* rarely meant anything good. He wanted to be a father to the twins, but was he about to reject her again?

That evening, despite their party excitement and valentine-candy-induced sugar shock, the twins fell asleep quickly. Frank helped get them ready for bed, relishing the opportunity that still felt so new to him. Then he went downstairs so they could have time alone with their mother.

He looked longingly at the couch and the TV remote. Man, he was tired.

He turned on the gas fireplace and then wandered into the kitchen. What would make this upcoming conversation with April easier?

He opened a cupboard and looked inside. Tea. She liked tea. He pulled out a couple of cups and two tea bags from a box labeled "Dreamland." Something to help them sleep, not keep them awake. Sleep had been in short supply these past few days.

He thought of something and reached into his coat pocket. There was the bag of foil-wrapped dark chocolate hearts that Olivia had pressed into his hand at the end of the party. *For your valentine*, she'd whispered with a sly smile.

He opened the bag and dumped its contents into a pretty bowl.

He found a radio station featuring old blues and jazz and turned it on, low.

And *then* he flopped onto the couch, clicked on the TV and checked the score of the hockey game. Pens weren't looking good for the playoffs, but there was time to turn it around.

He heard her coming down the stairs and muted the TV.

"You made tea," she said with a tired smile. "Thank you." She flopped down on the other end of the couch.

"Have some chocolate," he said, and held out the bowl to her.

"You don't have to ask me twice." She took a foil-wrapped heart.

He did, too. "You as tired as I am?"

"Totally." She let her head flop back against the couch. "I should hop on my laptop. See if there are any responses to the jobs I've applied for. But I'm worn-out."

"Same here," he said. "And at some point we need to deal with arrangements going forward. With the twins, I mean. How we'll manage child support, custody, stuff like that."

The word *custody* made her jerk around to face him. "You want custody?"

How to explain what he wanted? "We'll have to deal with those issues, along with figuring out why they already decided I'm their dad and told everyone."

She shook her head and rolled her eyes. "Right? I never, ever breathed a word of it to them. I was shocked to hear them say it."

"Me, too." He sighed. "Like I said, we need to deal with those issues. Right now, though, I feel like eating candy and watching sports."

"Let's do that." She grabbed the remote and turned on the hockey game.

And so they lounged, eating chocolate and drinking tea and cheering the Pens on to a surprise victory. After a fist bump, he grabbed her hand in his for a minute.

Pure impulse, but she didn't pull away.

He clicked off the TV and turned toward her, still holding her hand. "I'm sorry I was so panicked when I learned about the twins," he said. "I needed time to think, but I didn't mean to make you feel bad. You did the best you could in a hard situation."

She looked at him, blue-green eyes wide. "Thank you," she said. "And I'm sorry I didn't keep trying to find you and tell you that you were a father. I should have. I let my hurt feelings, and my fear of our parents, control me."

He shifted their clasped hands so their fingers interlocked. Her skin was soft, her grip strong.

Whatever had been simmering between them heated to a boil. Their eyes met and held. Her lips parted. Then she shook her head, smiling a little, and let out a breath. "So! What to do about the kids. That counselor has a Saturday-morning appointment available. Should I take it?"

"Absolutely. I have no idea how to handle them deciding I'm their dad without any facts to back it up."

"I don't know, Frank," she said. "They

354   *The Veteran's Valentine Helper*

do have *some* facts. Like you've tried to teach them things, and you've helped them when they were sick, and you've intro- duced them to a wonderful new extended family. Why wouldn't they at least *want* you to be their dad?"

Her words soothed something deep in- side, some fear that he wouldn't know how to parent and would morph into a replica of his father. "My brothers are all good fa- thers. Guess I learned a few things from them, not that I'd admit it to them."

"You're all good men," she said, her voice quiet.

A jazz version of "Moon River" came onto the radio. Wind shook the outside of the house, but here, inside, it was warm. Almost too warm. "These have been re- ally good days for me," he told her. "I've loved taking care of the kids."

"Even cleaning up when they've been sick?" she asked, one eyebrow raised.

"Well…that wasn't my favorite part." But he hadn't minded doing it. It had been a way to help the twins—and to help April, too, to lift some of her burden.

Suddenly, the soldier in him was impatient with delay and procrastination and euphemisms. He needed to speak his feelings, and he needed to do it now. He squeezed her hand. "I've never stopped caring for you, April," he said. "And I'm wondering…" Too late, he realized he'd dived in without knowing exactly where this conversation was going.

She was watching him steadily. "You're wondering what?"

He drew in a breath and went for it. "Is there a possibility that we could be together?"

She tilted her head. "In what way?"

Time to carry the ball to the finish line. "Like this." He waved a hand to encompass the room and the upstairs and the kitchen. "Like a family."

"You mean live together?" She frowned. "No. No way."

His heart sank, and it must have shown on his face.

"I'm sure it would be nice while it lasted," she said gently, "but a temporary arrangement wouldn't be right for the twins."

He wanted to smack himself in the head. "That's not what I meant. I'd want us to make a commitment."

She tilted her head a little. "It would be good for the kids if we all at least lived in the same town."

He nodded slowly. Did she want him around to be a dad for her kids, or did she feel something for him as a man? "Ideally, it would be more than just sharing custody across town," he said. "I've always wanted a family, if I could manage it right. Since we've gotten closer, that feeling...well, it's grown."

"Is this 'be together like a family' thing just for the kids?" she asked bluntly. "Or do you care for me?"

His heart rate picked up. She wouldn't ask that if she didn't care for him a little, would she? "It's partly about the kids, of course. They've brought us back together." But it was so, so much more. He turned to face her. "I'd want to be with you, kids or not. I love your resilience and your sense of humor. I love talking to you, being with you. I respect your intelligence and your strong faith." He touched her arm. "I also think you're incredibly beautiful."

She was staring at him like she was trying to read him. Her chest rose and fell quickly. And he knew that he wanted this. Wanted it more than he'd ever wanted anything in his life.

No time like the present. He took both her hands in his. "April, I want to explore what we have together, apart from the kids. I want us to think about a possible future together."

April froze, looking at Frank. His eyes were steady and sure, and his hands, holding hers, didn't waver. The music switched to another old love song. Heat from the fireplace wasn't the only reason she felt warm all over. This was intense.

What did she want? Could she trust him?

Men hadn't been good for her so far. Her dad, as much as she'd loved him, had hurt her deeply when he'd rejected her. Frank had hurt her by leaving, too.

He'd had his reasons, though. She understood that now. Just like she'd had her reasons for keeping her children's paternity a secret.

God, what do I do? Is this of You?

She sucked in a breath and looked at Frank's handsome face and nodded. Yes, she could take this leap of faith. She was strong enough now. And she believed in him, believed he was a good man, kind and safe and smart.

Any commitment was a risk, but she was willing to take that kind of risk now, with God's help. "I think," she said slowly, "I think it's worth a try."

"Let me turn it around. Do you think that because you want a dad for the kids, or because you want to be with me?" His gaze was steady, but there was vulnerability in his eyes.

She *did* want a dad for Evelyn and Eli, but that wasn't anywhere near the only reason she cared for him, and he needed to know that. She leaned forward and took his face in her hands and kissed him. "You're a good man, Frank Wilkins. Strong and kind and smart. *And* you're a hero. Any woman would be blessed to have you for a life partner, but I'm glad it's me you chose. Because yes, I want to be with you. For you."

The next little while was a haze of kissing and planning and sharing dreams, eating chocolate and drinking tea, laughing together. April had never felt such joy, pure joy, in her heart.

Thank You, Father, she prayed as she settled back in Frank's arms.

Epilogue

One year later, in the middle of their Valentine's Day wedding reception, April put her hands to flushed cheeks and leaned against a side wall of the cozy, candlelit barn where she'd just become a wife.

The wood interior glowed golden, and the floral centerpieces mingled pink and red and white flowers, simply gorgeous.

"I couldn't imagine how a winter wedding would work in a barn," Kelly said as she came up beside April, "but this is really nice."

"Helps to have a big play area for the kids," April said. They both looked over to the side area of the barn, where all the cousins ran around together, adorable in their rumpled dress-up clothes. Eli, his red vest hanging open, was leading a couple of the younger kids in some kind of a super-hero game. He'd really come into his own this past year, and having a good father as a role model had been a big help.

They hadn't taken that connection for granted. They'd all visited the family counselor in Uniontown individually, as well as making several visits as a family. Frank had taken things slowly with the kids. They'd had a few fights and tears, like any family, but they were making it work. "Thank you so much for being willing to take the kids during our honeymoon," she said to Kelly.

"Of course! Zinnia will love having them. Big kids for her to play with, instead of just her annoying baby brother." She gave April a quick side hug. "I'm so excited for you guys to take a riverboat cruise! What a treat!"

"We're excited." April waved as Kelly headed off toward a cluster of moms, all of whom April now counted as friends.

"That's because you're both history nerds." April's cousin Nadine had come up on her other side. She must have heard the honeymoon talk.

"Guilty." That was just one of the ways she and Frank were compatible. Instead of a sunny beach vacation, they'd both wanted a trip with a lot of history to enjoy. Short, so that the twins wouldn't be without them too long. An eight-day cruise of the lower Mississippi was perfect.

She had no doubt the trip would be educational, but she also knew it would be romantic. Very romantic. She looked across the room to where Frank stood talking with his father and brothers, Dozer at his side. Just seeing him, so handsome in his dark tux, made her heart pound faster.

She forced herself to turn away and focus on Nadine. "I hope you're having a good time."

"It's fine. I'm fine. I never expect to have a good time at weddings, but yours is nice." She gave April a hug and then hurried away before April could ask her what her cryptic statement meant.

Olivia and her sister came over to offer congratulations, and they chatted for a few minutes. The twins had moved on to a different classroom for second grade, but Olivia had remained a good friend. Her sister was nice, too, though harder to get to know. She looked a little melancholy. Combined with Nadine's remark, April was reminded that weddings could be painful for some. She resolved to include Olivia's sister in their next girls' night out. Nadine, too, and some of her new friends from the school where she was now working as a teacher's aide.

She stole another glance at Frank and caught him looking at her. He gave her a speculative smile that made her cheeks go hot. He beckoned her over.

Jodi came and walked beside her. Of all

her new sisters-in-law, Jodi had become her closest friend. They'd taken to writing together a couple of times a week, when Jodi could get a break from her new twins, and they always ended up talking a lot as well.

She made it to the Wilkins men's cluster and Frank held out an arm, pulled her close and kissed her soundly, making her blush and his brothers hoot and catcall. Dozer clambered to his feet and gave one deep bark.

"I got a beef with you," Frank's father said to her. "Another alcohol-free wedding. What's up with you people?"

He was kidding, but not, she could tell. Frank and his brothers exchanged glances.

But as it turned out, they didn't have to handle the situation, because Evelyn came marching over, pretty as a painting in her red velvet dress. She'd been a stunning flower girl and she knew it; there was a definite strut in her step. She bypassed Frank and April and went right for Mr.

Wilkins. "Grandpa," she said, taking his hand. "I want to dance with the big people. Will you dance with me?"

Mr. Wilkins's face went from slightly hostile to kind in an instant. "I sure will, honey," he said. They walked toward the dance floor hand in hand.

"She's got him so charmed," Jodi said. "I think she's his favorite grandchild."

April started to protest, but Jodi held up a hand. "It's fine. I'm not jealous. Evelyn has the perfect personality to get along with her grandpa."

Frank laughed. "She's the take-charge type, for sure."

"And that's just what Dad needs," Cam said. "We needed an Evelyn in the family."

"And an Eli," Jodi said quickly. "And an April."

"You're sweet." April hugged her friend.

There had been so many hugs today. So much fun. She and the twins were a part of the community and part of a large extended family, and she loved it.

Most of all, though, she loved her husband. He was everything she hadn't even known to dream of. She leaned against him, and he stroked her hair, and her heart felt full to overflowing.

It hadn't been easy, and it hadn't come to pass by human effort alone. She could feel God's hand in everything that had happened. Truly, He'd worked it all for good. She closed her eyes, leaned against Frank and whispered a heartfelt prayer of thanks.

* * * * *

If you enjoyed this
K-9 Companions book, be sure
to look for Rescue on the Farm
by Allie Pleiter,
available in March 2025, wherever
Love Inspired books are sold!

Dear Reader,

Thank you for reading another story set in Holiday Point, Pennsylvania! Frank is the last of the Wilkins brothers to get his happily-ever-after. Just to recap, here are all the previous Holiday Point stories:

Free online reads:

- *Nanny for the Summer* (Cam Wilkins's story, available free on Harlequin.com)
- *Summertime Secrets* (Holiday Point's church secretary and custodian fall in love, available free on Harlequin.com)

Full-length novels and novellas:

- *A Companion for Christmas* (Alec Wilkins's story)
- "A Mother for His Child" (Blake and Zoey's novella in *A Mother's Gift* anthology—Zoey is a waitress in the Holiday Point diner)
- *A Companion for His Son* (Olivia's story—she's Eli and Evelyn's teacher)

•*His Christmas Salvation* (Fisk Wilkins's story)

If you visit my website and sign up for my newsletter, you'll get all the details.

Don't forget, too, that there are a lot more K-9 Companions books by me and by other Love Inspired authors. They're available wherever books are sold, so if you're a dog lover, why not treat yourself to a few more stories of lovable service dogs and sweet romance?

Happy Valentine's Day,
Lee